Cuckoo Clock Caper

A Josephine Stuart Mystery

by

Joyce Oroz

For information, email **Cozy Cat Press**, cozycatpress@aol.com or visit our website at: www.cozycatpress.com

COZY CAT
P R E S S

ISBN: 978-1-939816-10-8
Printed in the United States of America

Cover design by Littera Designs
http://www.litteradesigns.com

1 2 3 4 5 6 7 8 9 10

I want to dedicate this book to my friend, Tomi Edmiston, who worked tirelessly at cleaning up my mistakes.

I want to thank Wendy Carter and Marlene Sherwin for their sharp red pencils and encouragement over the years. Many thanks to Avery Laurin, Michael Laurin and Jeff Holmbeck (my tech team) who saved my computer from owner induced destruction many times over. I especially want to thank the man who always believed in me, my husband, Art Oroz.

CHAPTER ONE

It was the best of times…and suddenly it was the worst of times, the night my neighbor's house blew up. Before that, my life was on cruise control with very few bumps or sharp turns in the road. I painted murals by day and socialized with my friends by night. Solow, my faithful basset, brought me a newspaper dripping with saliva each morning. Alicia Quintana, my best friend, invited me over for dinner at least once a week. Her ten-year-old son, Trigger, called me Auntie Jo, and her husband, Ernie, called me, Josephine. But David Galaz knew me best and called me Josie.

The explosion shook my bed, rattled the windows and sent books crashing into a heap on the floor. I leaped out of bed, tripped over the books and stumbled down the dark hall. A smaller second explosion pushed me off balance. My shoulder hit the wall. I staggered through the kitchen on wobbly legs and gazed out the living room window facing west.

There were ten homes west of my old adobe, each on five acres of grassland sprinkled with oak trees, wild lilac and poison oak. I knew by the red sky that a neighbor was in trouble.

Sirens shrieked up the road named after Otis somebody. I stared out the window, slack-jawed, heart pounding, listening to Solow's intense howls.

My only comfort was the fact that David lived in the other direction. He had a bigger house than mine, an apricot orchard and a cat named Fluffy who led my dog on many a futile chase. David had been divorced ever since his wife ran off with the preacher ten years ago. He had retired at age fifty-two with a nice pension from IBM. On the night of the explosion, he was visiting his son and granddaughter in Modesto, which meant Solow and I were on our own.

I opened the front door and stepped outside. The red glowing sky finally turned grey as smoke obscured the western stars. Even in daylight I would not have been able to see the actual fire because of the hilly topography between me and my neighbors. Most of the houses on Otis were positioned similar to mine at the end of long driveways. We were all close to having a view of the Pacific Ocean, but not quite.

I stood in the dark wondering which neighbor had lost their home. I knew them all fairly well, except for the people two doors down. No one knew them well but we all had heard the rumors. Mr. Hooley and his sister were older than the spring-loaded bed I inherited from my grandmother and probably older than the giant oak tree in my backyard. People said they never went to school, held a job or married. A picture of Ma and Pa Kettle popped into my mind. I had never really seen the Hooleys, just a couple of beat up hats riding low in the cab of a barely blue eighty-four Chevy pickup.

Solow took one sniff outside and high-tailed it back to his doggie bed across the room from my bed. I followed Solow's example of self-control. At first my pillow felt comforting but that didn't last long. I tossed and turned, wrestling with my innate curiosity. Whose house exploded and why?

I clicked the lamp on.

"Solow, wake up. You want to go for a ride?"

He looked at me as if I'd been eating wild mushrooms. He dropped his head and closed his eyes.

"Come on. I'm going for a ride."

Solow finally raised his head as I pulled on a robe and shoved my feet into slippers. He followed me through the house and out the front door. The smell of smoke sat heavy in the air. Stars were visible in the eastern sky only.

I gave Mr. Chubby a boost into the passenger seat of my middle-aged red Mazda pickup and turned the key. Solow drooled with anticipation as we made a tight circle, crunched down the gravel driveway and turned left onto Otis.

The one-lane road made three turns before we saw glowing embers rising above wild lilac bushes fronting the Hooley property. I cautiously made a left turn onto the Hooley's asphalt driveway, drove a hundred yards and parked in the grass behind three fire engines. I recognized the frame of a burned out '84 Chevy pickup, still smoking near the glowing, collapsing framework of a two-story house.

A fireman aimed water at the big black pile. Water turned to white steam that billowed upward toward a mournful moon. Three firemen loaded the trucks with equipment, preparing to leave. There were no other signs of life.

Suddenly a face appeared in my window. As my head snapped to the left, Solow let out an ear-splitting howl.

The fireman outside my window motioned for me to roll the window down. When I came to my senses and did what I was told, he politely told me to leave the property.

"I'm worried about my neighbors. Are they OK?"

"I'm sorry, Ma'am, we haven't seen anyone. We really can't say much at this point."

"I'll move my truck right away...but can you tell me what caused the explosion?"

"You heard an explosion?"

I nodded. "Two of them. The first one shook my bed."

"Interesting," he said over his shoulder as he took off up the hill toward the action.

I turned my truck around and two minutes later we were home. Under normal circumstances, I would have sat for a minute enjoying the balmy, starry night. But that night was different. I wanted to forget the charred mess I had seen. I hoped and prayed the Hooleys were OK, somehow, somewhere.

Solow followed me into my dark house. We felt our way to the bedroom and crashed in our beds. Solow was snoring in his bed before the sheet hit my chin.

I dreamt about two little hoot owls sitting on a branch in a eucalyptus tree. A crowd of people looked up and taunted the birds, daring them to fly; but the birds made it known that they were afraid to leave the tree. A raccoon shimmied up the tree trunk and began swinging from branch to branch. One of the birds panicked and fell head first onto a rock below.

I looked up and noticed that the second bird was missing.

It was Thursday morning, four days before my next mural job was due to start. I rolled over, yawned and suddenly remembered what seemed like a nightmare. But when I sorted it out in my mind, I realized the terrible fire had really happened. The Hooleys had lost their home. I heard a noise. Solow wasn't in the room so I rolled out of bed, pulled on my robe and shuffled down the hall to the kitchen.

Solow stood by the backdoor wagging his tail, waiting to go outside.

"OK, big guy...out you go." I watched him race after David's furry white cat. Fluffy hopped through the deep grass like a short-eared bunny, and Solow galloped along behind. A few minutes later my basset was back, breathing hard, staring at the door with his tongue hanging loose. I let him in and laughed out loud.

I jumped when I heard an echo—a laugh behind my back, and spun around, fists raised in a defensive posture.

"Who are you?" I shrieked.

"Emmett," the man said calmly as he took a step back. He was my height, about five-seven, but stringy, wrinkled and bent. He had a long narrow nose, dark eyes under fluffy white brows, a lower tooth missing and an Einstein scramble of white hair on top of his head. He wore an old leather vest over his wrinkled long sleeved shirt. His pants puddled over bare feet. Pa Kettle had nothing on this guy.

"How did you get in here? I didn't hear anyone knock," I snarled.

"The door wasn't locked...."

"What are you doing in my house?" I put my hands on my hips and tried to look seriously mean, but the old coot wasn't buying it.

"Your door wasn't locked and I needed a place to sleep."

"What are you talking about? You're not making sense. Maybe I should call the police."

"Please, Ma'am, no police." Solow sidled over to the man for a backrub. "You have a nice home here and a good dog."

"Looks like you and Solow know each other. What's going on anyway?" I tried to ignore one of my favorite rules of life—if Solow likes you, you must be OK.

"Yes, we know each other. He's been to my house before."

"Where is your...is it up this road?" He nodded. "Don't tell me it's the one that...."

"...burned down last night." He stroked the stubble on his chin.

An icy feeling swept through my body. I shivered.

"Mr. Hooley, sit down. I'm so sorry you lost your house. Where's your sister?"

He looked at the floor.

"She didn't come out of the house," he groaned, dropping into a chair.

An even bigger chill hit me and lasted much longer.

"You spent the night...?"

"...on the couch. I like the fancy little pillow and the quilt was very nice."

"Why did you come to my house? I don't even know you."

"You're the only neighbor who doesn't lock your door," he smiled.

"I have a guard dog but maybe I'll lock-up from now on. Are you hungry?"

"I can wait. I could boil coffee for you," he said, with a slight accent. European, but I wasn't sure which country.

"Boil? Ah, I'll just put Mr. Coffee to work and you can pour yourself a cup in no time." I left the coffee to perk and hurried to my room to get dressed. I decided to dress first and put the books away later. I jumped into cut-off Levis and a blouse, ran a comb through my unruly auburn hair and gave my teeth a quick brushing.

I didn't feel completely comfortable leaving a strange man alone in my kitchen, but I felt sorry for him at the same time. Even though he'd entered my house and slept on my sofa, I couldn't really blame him for trespassing. He'd lost his sister and his home. Maybe he was disoriented or had a bad case of dementia or amnesia or something.

I entered the kitchen. "I see that Solow brought you the newspaper."

Emmett nodded as he drank coffee and read the saliva-soaked paper out loud to Solow.

I began preparing breakfast, glad to be helping Mr. Hooley in his time of sorrow.

Solow skipped his morning nap, preferring to listen to the old man read. There was no mention of a fire in the newspaper. After all, it had happened just five hours earlier. It would probably be Friday's headline.

The phone rang. I smiled at the sound of David's voice.

"Josie, honey, sorry I didn't call last night. Things were pretty crazy around here. Harley had to make an insurance house call. One of his clients ran his truck off the road, over a sidewalk and into a bar."

"Same bar he left?" I laughed. "So what did you and Monica do?"

"I played fairy princess with Monica until Harley came home. My back is killing me, right where my wings are supposed to be. So what's happening with you?"

"David, you won't believe it! There was an explosion last night. It shook my bed and then there was a big fire up the street. It was three in the morning, but you know me, I had to go see for myself so Solow and I…."

"That's nice, sweetie. I'm afraid Monica, I mean the fairy princess, is calling me. Gotta run. I'll call tonight." We hung up and I turned my attention to making breakfast.

"Hilda always made the porridge," Emmett said.

"I can make oatmeal if that's what you want. I'll share the waffles with Solow."

"Oh no, no, I don't like porridge. I never told Hilda that."

"Why didn't you tell her? Maybe she'd have cooked other things for you, like bacon and eggs or...."

"...biscuits and gravy. She only made food from the old country. Our mother taught her to make schnitzel, matzo balls and cheese blintzes. Hilda didn't want to learn American ways, but I like the American hamburger." He ran his boney thumb up and down the mug handle, eyes focused on the wall.

I never had a sister, but if I lost one I knew I'd have been devastated. Poor Mr. Hooley must have been out of his mind with grief.

"I need to buy groceries today. Would you like to come along? Might do you good to get out in the sunshine...."

"...and see people at the store."

"Do you always finish other people's...."

"...sentences? Just Hilda's." A quick smile flickered across his ancient lips.

"How old was your sister?"

"Eighty-seven. I'm two years older." He dug into his waffle and bacon like a man who'd eaten mush for breakfast his whole life.

"What else did Hilda cook for you?"

"She made pea soup mostly. Sometimes she made potato or noodle with cheese. She was a fine cook. She and I and our mother left Germany and went to

Venezuela just before the big war started. Two years later we came to America."

I sized him up and decided he must have avoided the army sixty or seventy years ago. Emmett was ten years older than my folks. Mom and Dad were creeping up on eighty, but still moving in the fast lane. They moved from zumba to ballroom dancing to camping, fishing, hiking, and bowling at the Bowl and Bowl.

"Don't worry about the dishes. I'll take care of them. You just relax," I said, taking a dirty dish out of Emmett's shaky hands. "Do you want me to drive you over to your house…ah, where your house was?"

Emmett hung his head and stared at the floor.

"That's all right. We'll do it some other time." I gave Solow his kibble, loaded the dishwasher and swept the floor. Poor Emmett didn't even have a floor or a house or a sister. A lump formed in my throat, the kind that shows up every time I have seriously sad thoughts.

"Ma'am…."

"My name is Josephine."

"Josephine, when you go to the store, would you buy a toothbrush for me?"

"Sure, but aren't you going with me?"

Looking dour, Emmett shook his head and shuffled out of the room. Solow followed him into the living room, probably hoping for another backrub. The next time I saw them, Emmett was stretched out on the couch sound asleep and Solow was curled up on the floor next to his friend.

Normally, I would not leave my house with a stranger in it but I already felt like Emmett was a friend. As I walked out the front door, Solow's eyes followed me. Surprisingly, he didn't stand up and whine to be taken for a ride. He just lay there, protecting and comforting his pal.

I drove the ten miles to Watsonville out of habit, letting my mind wander back to the terrible fire scene, the charred pile of beams, the river rock fireplace standing alone and puffs of grey smoke reaching for the moon. I wondered if Emmett was in shock.

I drove into the grocery store parking lot, cut the engine and pulled my mind back into the business of shopping. I caught up to my friend, Robert, who was busy shoving half a dozen shopping carts into their corral.

"Hi, Robert, what's up?"

"Josephine, didn't see you there. I hear your neighborhood had some excitement last night. What's it all about?"

"I was going to ask you the same question. You always seem to know what's going on." It was true. My young freckled friend read the paper and listened to KPIG radio and watched KPUT TV news. He was half my age but I admired his inquiring mind.

"I'll see you at the check out," Robert said as he followed me into the store wearing a big blue apron that should have been shorter and wider for a proper fit. He turned left toward the check out.

I turned right to the dog food aisle. I loaded my cart with forty pounds of kibble, two boxes of frozen waffles, a dozen eggs, salad fixings and a toothbrush. After that I hit the meat department pretty hard, threw in a loaf of bread and topped the pile with ice cream and chocolate sprinkles. My intention was to gather up thousands of tasty calories for my skinny friend, Emmett.

"Josephine, tell me about the fire," Robert said as he ran a box of tissues over the scanner. "I heard it was on Otis and I was worried about you." He began bagging my groceries, completely engrossed in my explosion and fire story. He automatically loaded the grocery bags into my cart, shoved the sack of kibble onto the lower shelf and pushed the cart outside to my truck.

I told Robert about Mr. Hooley showing up in my kitchen, giving me a good scare. He laughed when I put up my dukes to show how I had reacted to Mr. Hooley's voice.

"This Hooley guy is how old?"

"He says he's close to ninety…but he totally surprised me…you had to be there. So, Robert, what did you hear on KPIG?"

"They said no one was in the house at the time of the fire." He looked at me and cocked his head. "You know something, don't you, Jo?"

"Apparently Emmett's sister was in the house." I glanced at my foot, feeling the lump lodging itself in my throat again. "The poor man's in a daze right now."

Robert nodded. "Have the police come around yet?" he asked.

I shook my head. "See ya later, Robert." I fired up the truck and pointed it toward the foothills. As soon as I had time, I called the County Sheriff's Department and let them know that Mr. Hooley would be staying with me for awhile.

CHAPTER TWO

Friday morning I woke up determined to find out why the Hooley house had blown up, sending Emmett's younger sister, Hilda, to Saint Peter's pearly gates before her time. I had asked a few questions the day before but the old man wasn't making sense. He didn't want to see the remains of his house. He seemed content to watch reruns on TV all day.

I was far from content. I wanted to know why a house would suddenly blow up in the middle of the night, and how did Emmett escape uninjured? I pondered these questions as I cleared the breakfast dishes, mopped the floor and threw a basket of dirty clothes into the washing machine. The day was warming up nicely. I offered Emmett a ride to his property, but he declined, keeping his eyes on the TV screen.

"OK, Solow, do you want to go for a walk?" I waved a biscuit treat in front of his sensitive nose. He looked at Emmett, then the treat. Finally he stood up took the treat and sauntered out the front door.

Solow and I pounded the pavement around three turns in the road, made a left at the Hooley mailbox and trudged up Emmett's long blacktopped driveway. We stopped beside the only standing remnant of his house, a giant river rock fireplace, and stood for a moment of complete silence. Various chunks of blackened walls leaned against each other on top of burnt timbers sprinkled with broken glass and melted hardware. The foul air was still, no birds sang, no sound came from the ridge where a long row of eucalyptus trees usually whispered in the breeze. Silently, turkey buzzards cut circles in the overly blue sky.

The string of eucalyptus trees behind my house stretched along the ridge, cutting through several properties including the Hooley backyard. The trees formed a line about two-hundred feet up the hill from the burnt homestead. Halfway between the ashes and the very tall eucalyptus was a scattering of oak trees, half a dozen young redwoods and a few Monterey pines. I hurried to keep up with Solow as he sniffed his way up the hill and howled when he came to an area of thick vegetation, mostly wild lilac, bottlebrush and Laurel. He circled the area, and then disappeared through a break in the matted foliage.

"Solow, come on boy, let's go home." There was no sign of him, so I squeezed through a narrow space between the bushes into an open area surrounding a cottage covered in grey shingles. The door was wide open and Solow had already entered the little cabin.

I stood in the doorway and called Solow. The place had a piney smell, like Mr. Hooley. Two multi-paned windows in the roof served as skylights, sending sunlight to a floor littered with cut logs. As my eyes adjusted to the dim light, I realized I was looking at a mixture of firewood for the potbellied stove, and wood that had been carved and painted. There were carved birds and animals as well as figures of people with smiling faces wearing colorful, old-world clothing.

"Solow, look at this mess! Looks like a giant cuckoo clock explosion." Not wishing to fall on my face, I stood still in a sea of broken wood carvings—

painted and unpainted. There were mallets, knives, chisels and clock parts scattered here and there. Two unscathed cuckoo clocks hung at a tilt on the opposite wall surrounded by dozens of empty hooks. I could only imagine how scary the explosion had been.

I noted the narrow cot against one wall and a blanket tossed to the floor. Across the room, there was a small sink and a workbench with a vice. An ornately carved wooden box sat on the floor near my foot. I opened it, exposing a full set of woodworking tools. The inside of the lid had been engraved with lines of script in a foreign language.

Solow gingerly climbed over the dismembered clocks, straight to a large bone under the sink on the other side of the room. He picked it up with his teeth and brought it back to show me.

"You act like that's your bone. Did Emmett give it to you?"

Solow carried his bone out the door and all the way home. I watched him from behind as he pranced down the street on thick bouncy legs. His ears flapped up and down and strings of saliva dribbled off the bone.

I opened my front door and heard the gentle snores of a man catching up on sleep.

Solow dropped his bone next to the couch and waited for Emmett to wake up.

I grabbed the phone, scurried out the backdoor and dialed my best friend, Alicia.

"You sound strange, Jo. What's going on?"

"My neighbor's house blew up last night, and he's staying here with me."

"That's awful! Obviously it's not David you're talking about. Who is it? Is he competition for David?"

I laughed. "Not really. Mr. Hooley is one wrinkle short of ninety. I think he whittles."

"Most old people do."

"No, Allie, he whittles on wood, you know, carves it."

"Sorry, I think my phone is cutting out. Before it dies, are you coming for dinner tonight? Trigger's really counting on it. Bring your friend. I'm dying to know why his house blew up."

We hung up and I called David. He answered in his fairy princess voice, and then cleared his throat. He told me he was having tea with Monica. I pictured him sitting in a child's chair, knees tucked under his chin, brown eyes trained on the five-year-old with flaming red hair and a smile that could warm a whole pot of tea.

"David, did I tell you I have a houseguest?"

"No, who is she?"

"Mr. Hooley. Remember, I told you his house blew up?"

"I think I'd have remembered that. The name sounds familiar."

"He's our neighbor. Unfortunately, we think his sister didn't survive the fire. I think Emmett is still in shock. All he wants to do is sleep."

"Probably the best thing for him. How old did you say he is?"

"Eighty-nine. He whittles, I mean, he carves wooden cuckoo clocks."

"I can't wait to hear the rest of your story. If Harley gets home in time I'll drive straight to Watsonville and meet you at Alicia's. It's not every day Trigger turns ten and a half." We laughed. Alicia had only one child, and one birthday party a year wasn't enough for her. Trigger's real birthday was November sixth, but May sixth was celebrated as a half-birthday—one more excuse to eat cake and celebrate a very special young man.

We hung up and I trundled down the hall to the bedroom. I began putting books back on the shelf. While I was at it, I dusted and sorted and finally was able to part with two books. I planned to give them to Alicia or Mom...I couldn't just get rid of them completely. Books and family photographs were sacred possessions.

I heard someone knocking at the front door and rushed through the house to answer it.

Emmett sat up on the couch and rubbed his eyes.

I opened the door.

Two deputy sheriffs asked to come in.

I stepped back, Emmett yawned and Solow wagged his tale. I introduced Deputy Denise Lund, a rangy blond with ice-blue eyes, and Deputy Calvin Sayer, an older, thicker, more relaxed African-American officer. I knew the sheriff's deputies from a previous encounter.

Emmett stood up and tipped his head.

"I'm Emmett Hooley. Are you folks looking for me?" he asked, teetering side to side.

"Mr. Hooley," Officer Lund began. "We're investigating the accident at 500 Otis, Wednesday night. Were you at home when the house caught fire?"

I asked everyone to sit and took the rocker for myself.

"Yes, we were at home, Officer," Emmett said, looking alert for the first time all day.

Sayer checked his notepad. "You live with your sister, Hilda Hooley?"

"Yes sir, for the last thirty-two years." Emmett cleared his throat. "It was a good house."

"Where is your sister?" Lund asked.

"Where people go when they die," he said.

Lund cocked her head. "Mr. Hooley, are you saying your sister is dead?"

My rocker sped up.

"My sister was in the house when the explosion hap...."

"Explosion? What explosion?" Sayer asked.

"The explosion I felt all the way down here in my house," I said. "It knocked all the books off my shelf."

Lund squinted in my direction and jotted something down.

"Do you know what happened to your sister, sir?"

"I only know she did not come out of the house," Emmett sighed.

I wished I could hug him and prop him up with kind words. My rocker sped up as Officer Lund narrowed her eyes.

"Sir, why didn't you report this to the authorities?"

"I believe I just did," Emmett said.

Solow picked up his bone, left my side and curled up on the old man's feet. Maybe he was afraid of the rocker or maybe he felt sorry for Mr. Hooley. Either way, he made Emmett smile for a second.

Officer Sayer walked to the door.

Lund stood and announced there would be an investigation and warned us not to leave town.

I closed the door behind them, enjoying the silence.

Emmett pulled his feet up on the couch and lowered his mass of white hair onto the red silk throw pillow Mom had given me a few months earlier for my fiftieth birthday.

I made grilled cheese sandwiches hoping Emmett would smell them and come running. He didn't open his eyes so I left him alone. Three hours later, I set a sandwich and a cup of hot tea on the coffee table in front of him and shook his boney shoulder.

He opened one eye. "Is something wrong, Josephine?"

"I think you should eat something, that's all. Are you feeling all right?"

He pulled away the lap blanket and slowly sat up. "I dreamt my house burned down," he said. "I can't seem to get away from it, so I guess I'll walk up there and look at what's left."

"I'll give you a ride in my...."

"...truck. That would be wonderful. Thank you, Josephine. I was wondering if I might rent a room from you for a little while...until I build a new house, that is?"

"A lumpy springy bed in the loft is all I have. Don't you have relatives you can go to?"

He shook his head. "Last night I slept very well in your house." He took a sip of tea. For some reason fate had sent the old man to me so I figured I better help out, even if it meant putting up with a houseguest. I wondered how long it would take to build a new house.

Emmett finished half of his sandwich and then we piled into the truck for a very short ride. Solow curled up under the dash on top of Mr. Hooley's bare feet, and two minutes later it was time to climb out. There was a tinge of burnt something in the air. I watched Emmett's reaction. Actually, there was no noticeable reaction. He just looked old and pale.

I followed Emmett as he circled the black remains of a house I had never seen.

"How old was your house?" I asked, figuring it was probably small and ancient like mine.

"Thirty-two years old. Hilda and I had it built after Mother died. She left us a fortune, you know."

"No, I didn't know. That's nice. How big was the house?"

"It was two stories, all redwood with a porch that wrapped around the front and another in the back. Hilda carved the front door in the old style...."

My jaw dropped. "Hilda carved the door?"

"Oh, yes, she carved a green man on the door, you know, a face with leaves coming out in all directions?"

"Ah, sure." I made a mental note to Google green man.

"Hilda carved posts for the stair rail and pillars in the library." He kicked a charred board with his foot. My next house will be smaller, and no embellishments from my...."

"...sister," I whispered, wondering what kind of gal does all that carving. I also wondered about the so-called fortune Emmett had inherited. I watched him turn his back and trudge up the path with Solow at his bare heels.

I caught up to the boys when the path took a turn around the vegetable garden and several fruit trees. I was right behind them as they walked through an opening in the dense ring of bushes.

Emmett stepped into the cottage and groaned.

I grabbed his elbow, thinking he might keel over.

Solow seemed right at home as he investigated under the sink, probably hoping the bone fairy had left him something tasty.

Emmett took a couple careful barefoot steps, picked up the wooden box of carving tools and cradled it in his arms as if it were a baby. A tear meandered down his cheek.

I turned away and waited outside, exploring the inner circle with its flower gardens backed up to the shingled cottage walls. Hand-carved wooden gnomes posed among the plants and a hammock hung from a giant oak tree. When I ran out of gnomes to look at, I peeked in the door to see how Mr. Hooley was doing. The poor man was stretched out on his cot, sound asleep.

I heard distant noises.

Solow poked his head outside. With a little encouragement, he followed me down the hill, past the orchard to the burnt rubble. The County Fire Inspector's SUV was parked next to a Sheriff's patrol car. I spotted Deputy Lund following the inspector. He wore gloves and talked into a recorder. They walked a wide circle, eyes to the ground, just inside the crime tape that Officer Sayer was posting around the ashes.

Sayer looked up as I approached.

"Ms. Stuart, I saw your truck. What brings you here?" Officer Sayer asked.

"Mr. Hooley wanted to check on his vegetable garden and pick up his mail. I don't think he's taking things very well."

"And Mr. Hooley is….?" Sayer looked behind me at a row of tomato plants thirty feet away.

"Oh, he's up there somewhere checking out the rest of his property." I thumbed the hilly five acres.

Solow sniffed Sayer's pants and shoes and was rewarded with a quick ear-rub.

"What have you found so far?" I asked, kicking a twisted, blackened metal window frame.

Before Sayer could answer, Deputy Lund marched over to us looking like she had swallowed a bug.

"Ms. Stuart, what are you doing here?"

"I was wondering if you found anything. Is this a crime scene?"

"As you can see we are conducting an investigation, so don't touch anything. We will let Mr. Hooley know if we find his sister's remains." She turned and fell back in step with the investigator.

Sayer rolled his eyes discreetly.

"You heard the officer. I think you should take Mr. Hooley away from here."

"Yeah, OK. I'll snag him." Solow got the memo and led me up the hill. I found Emmett asleep on the hammock outside the cottage and gave him a little shake.

"Mr. Hooley, wake up—we gotta get out of here."

He rolled his head my way. "Josephine, I thought you went home."

"I wouldn't leave you, Emmett. But I'm afraid the deputy sheriffs want us to leave right now." I grabbed his arm as he stood up on shaky legs. I looked around and sighed. "Don't worry, we'll come back when the officers are gone," I said, as we walked across the inner circle, squeezed through the hedge and followed the dirt path down to the ash pile.

By the time we piled into my truck, a red van and another sheriff's car had arrived. I drove to the end of the driveway, collected the mail and turned right onto Otis.

"Josephine, you didn't tell them about my...."

"Cottage...? Don't worry, I said you were roaming around in the back yard. It's pretty cool how the trees and bushes have totally surrounded the building."

"That was Hilda's idea. She liked her privacy. She spent many hours in that room carving her figurines while I made the clocks. Ironic, isn't it. We had a big house but spent most of our time in the little cottage."

"Emmett, did you sell...?"

"...cuckoo clocks?" He nodded. "We mailed clocks to people all over the world. We didn't need the money—it just gave us something to do. I have been making clocks my whole life, except when I was sixteen. That year my father arranged for the family to leave Germany because things were not going well for our people."

"Are you Jewish?"

"My mother, sister and I were German Jews, but my father was not Jewish. He worked in a brewery in Stuttgart. He heard rumors that bad things were happening to the Jews and put together a plan for us to escape to Switzerland. He wanted my family to leave the country together but just as we were about to go, two men from the brewery came to our house to take Papa back to work. There was a mechanical problem only my father knew how to fix. If he had not gone, the Nazis would have been suspicious and kept all of us from leaving. As it was, we had to leave in the night with only a few possessions."

"What happened to your father?"

"We never knew exactly." Emmet looked at the floor. "The Nazis probably punished him when we disappeared. We never heard from him." Emmett rubbed his chin, staring straight ahead. "Where was I? Oh yes…we traveled on foot every night and hid in the woods during daylight hours for over a week…all the way to Lake Constance on the border. We hid in the forest for a couple days until we found a fisherman willing to take us across the lake."

"Did you have to pay him to take you?"

"I remember my mother handing him something from her jewel case. We waited until it was dark. Another runaway Jew about my age arrived from Frankfurt and joined us on the little fishing boat. From the boat, we set foot on Swiss soil with great relief. The four of us walked another forty miles to Zurich where my father's brother, Uncle Lamar, lived."

"Did your uncle help you?"

"Yes…yes, he did. His son, my cousin, worked as a pilot flying freight into Switzerland from Spain and

Portugal. I only wish all the Jews could have had our luck. We stayed with Uncle Lamar's family over night and then he flew us on his regular route to Portugal. From Portugal we eventually took a boat to Venezuela. Two years later, we entered the USA and settled in San Jose, California." Emmett looked tired.

"I want to hear more of your stories but let's take a break for lunch first." I worked fast making sandwiches before Emmett had time to fall asleep again. He ate a few bites of his sandwich and sipped his hot tea. I tried to interest him in an old movie, but his dull eyes closed and the snoring began.

CHAPTER THREE

I stared at my book, not seeing a word of the complicated mystery. I had my own mystery to work on. I glanced over at Emmett on the sofa with his eyes closed and mouth open. I made a vow to myself to take him shopping for clothes.

I finally gave up, put my book down and turned on the computer. I wanted to know if Hooley was a common name. Were there any more Hooleys out there—relatives maybe. After a bit of investigation, I learned there were not many Hooleys around, other than an Irish pub.

It was five o'clock Friday afternoon, time to drive to Alicia's house for dinner. I ran a brush through my hair and quickly ironed my blue and white bargain blouse—the one David always commented on. The print went well with my white peddle pushers and flip flops. I checked the mirror, decided I was good to go and hurried into the living room to round up Mr. Hooley.

"Emmett...Emmett...Mr. Hooley. Oh good, you're awake." He sat up, looked around and yawned.

"What can I do for you, Josephine?"

"We're invited to my friend's house for dinner, remember?"

"You go ahead, I have some, ah, work to do."

I wished he would go with me, but his jaw was set as he waved me out the door. At least Solow would have company.

I deposited Trigger's half-birthday present in the passenger seat, drove to Watsonville and parked in front of Alicia's two-story house overlooking Drew Lake. The lake water covered about twenty acres. Lawns, boat docks, little sandy beaches and willows ringed the body of fresh water. Mallards, egrets, coots, Canadian geese and the occasional canoe called it home.

Trigger met me at the door and took his package.

"How's my favorite ten-year-old?"

"Ten and a half," Trigger corrected me. He looked at the wrapped, round gift and politely pretended not to know what it was.

"Thank you, Auntie Jo. Mama burned the enchiladas and now she's making more."

"Is she upset about that?"

"No, she sent Daddy to the store for more tortillas." Trigger took my hand and pulled me inside.

I immediately smelled burnt food. We found Alicia in the kitchen chipping black gunk off the baking pan with a spatula.

She looked up. "Jo, where's your gentleman friend?"

"Right here," a voice behind me said. I turned and received a kiss on my cheek from David.

Ernie was right behind David with a bag of tortillas from the store.

"Yeah, where is that mysterious man you told us about? How old did you say he is?"

"About eighty-nine," I said, "but he's in pretty good shape for being so old. Emmett told me he had some work to do but I think he's too depressed to do much of anything. I think that's why he wouldn't come with me tonight. I'm a little worried about him. Can I help you with anything, Allie?"

"I made this mess, now I'm going to fix it, but you can help Trigger set the table."

"Allie, what happened? You never burn food."

"I didn't hear the oven timer because I was outside trying to catch a wild goose with his feet tangled up in a fishing net." She stirred the sauce bubbling on the stove. "He was really hard to catch, even though he was tied up in that mess. Trigger threw a beach towel over the goose and I held him down while Trigger ran in the house and brought back scissors. We cut him free and watched him waddle down to the water. That's when Ernie came home from work and gave me the bad news about our dinner."

"Don't worry, Allie, we have all evening. Solow has been fed and he's very happy to be with Emmett."

"But you said you were worried about Emmett."

"He'll be all right—he has Solow." Everyone smiled and nodded. Solow usually had that effect on people. We sat on the deck observing two geese, dozens of ducks and a reflection of hills turning pink as we waited for the oven timer to announce dinner.

Dinner was finally served. It was worth waiting for but I was beyond starving. The before-dinner veggies and dip hadn't made a dent in my appetite. Some people can go for hour and hours without eating. I was never one of them. David and Alicia knew I had to eat to keep the grumpies away. My mind wandered back to Mr. Hooley, asleep in the little cottage. I finally realized I wasn't feeling grumpy, I was feeling sad.

"Jo, you seem distant," Alicia said. "Everything all right?"

"I was just thinking about poor old Emmett. I saw him asleep on his cot in the shack. He looked so alone and he doesn't even have a change of clothes. Everything is gone."

"If that's the case, we'll buy him some clothes tomorrow," David said, patting my arm gently.

Alicia and Ernie cleared the table. When they came back, Ernie was carrying a flaming chocolate cake. Trigger blew out the candles and cut five slices. As we indulged in chocolate bliss, he opened his three presents. One soccer ball from me, one basketball from David and a new baseball bat from his mom and dad.

"Trigger, now that you're officially ten and a half, we need to go home…and check on things."

David and I exchanged hugs all around and then piled into our separate vehicles. The stars were out and the road was mostly vacant. My mind wandered back to the shack full of clock pieces. Why was Emmett on the cot the night of the explosion? Did he get along with his sister? Was the explosion an accident?

I pulled to a stop in front of my house with David's headlights shining into my rearview mirror. I climbed out, ready for a little romance.

"You look beautiful in the moonlight, Josie." David wrapped his arms around me.

"You look pretty wonderful yourself…did you hear that?"

"Yeah, sounded like furniture or something." David was already ten paces ahead of me. He opened the front door.

Solow howled and I hurried to catch up.

David rushed across the living room, dodged a kitchen chair lying on its side and grabbed Emmett's dangling legs.

"Josie, get a knife!" I ran to the kitchen. No time to think about which knife was the sharpest. I already knew that none of them had been sharpened in some time. I grabbed a serrated steak knife and dashed up to the loft, heart pounding, legs shaking.

"Don't go wobbly on me, Jo. I'll hold him up—you cut the rope!"

"I'm trying…it's so thick…and this knife isn't very…OK, I'm getting it." Sweat poured down my face.

Emmett's face was turning blue.

My heart pounded even harder. "Hang on, Emmett, almost done. There you go." Lying on my belly, I reached between the rails and held his arms until he was too low for me to reach. By that time David had Emmett's limp body in his arms. He eased the old man onto the sofa.

I ran for the phone and dialed 911. "The paramedics will be here in a couple minutes. Is he breathing?"

"Barely." David gently lifted Emmett's head and slipped a pillow under the bushy white hair.

I covered him with a lap blanket while Solow licked a limp hand.

Suddenly two dark blue uniforms rushed into the room and bent over Mr. Hooley. One young man hooked Emmett up to oxygen while the other checked his eyes and reflexes. One of them turned his head and caught sight of the ugly rope lying on the floor.

We answered a few questions like, "What happened here?"

I mumbled something about Emmett getting tangled up in a rope.

The EMT looked at me funny and suggested Emmett go to the hospital.

Mr. Hooley sat up and said he absolutely would not go.

The paramedics packed up and left.

"Emmett, are you OK now?" I asked.

He nodded. "I'll be fine. I was depressed because I thought it was all my fault that Hilda died. Then I changed my mind. I was holding onto the rope, trying to loosen the knot when the chair tipped over."

"How could it be your fault?"

"I thought maybe I left the stove on or something...I didn't know what. But Hilda told me it wasn't my fault and to go find the murderer."

"But, how could you talk to...I mean, she's dead." I scratched my head.

David shook his head and looked at the ceiling.

Emmett glanced across the room where a short piece of rope hung from the banister. He rubbed his scrawny throat.

"The chair slipped and I couldn't hold on. It was a strange thing. I couldn't breath but I felt good—light as a feather," he smiled a crooked smile. "I was just about to follow the light out of this world when Hilda came to me. She convinced me that I should stay here and expose her murderer. I was just about to ask her who the murderer was when you folks cut me down."

"Did she tell you if the murderer was a he or a she? How they did it? Any clues at all?"

Emmett shook his head.

"Call me if you need me." David kissed me on my cheek and said goodnight.

Solow walked him to the door.

It was obvious to me that Emmett had changed his mind about going to heaven any time soon. His feelings of guilt had been erased and there was a twinkle in his eye I hadn't seen before. He was on a mission. He had something to do and I silently vowed to help him any way I could.

I told the old man about the shopping trip David and I planned for the next day.

Emmett actually cocked his head, smiled and looked down at his bare feet.

"I would like to buy a pair of shoes."

"We'll buy you a fine pair of shoes tomorrow, and clothes too. By the way, are there any more Hooleys living around here?"

"I don't personally know anyone in America by that name."

"So you don't have any relatives....?"

"Hooley is the name my family took when we left Germany. We had papers made in Switzerland because we were afraid of being arrested," Emmet yawned. "We wanted to immigrate like the Irish and the only Irishman we knew was Mick Hooley, my cousin's co-pilot. We didn't know very much about America and freedom. After a few years passed, we finally relaxed a bit, but we kept the name."

"What was your name in the old country?"

"Hymiller. My father brewed the best beer in Stuttgart. His father, my grandfather, gave him a special recipe which he gave to me just before we left on our journey to America. I keep it with me always."

"Did it burn...?"

"Oh, no. Like I said, I keep it with me," he smiled.

"Did you go into the beer business?"

"No, it didn't interest me. I kept the recipe and planned to sell it if I needed money someday. In the old country I worked for a clockmaker beginning at age eleven. I have always loved making clocks and Hilda loved to carve the ornamentation. We rented a small storefront in San Jose. Eventually we expanded into a larger store with three jewelry stores in other locations." He looked up at my pathetically cheap yellowed-plastic clock hanging on the wall. "You could use a good clock, Josephine," he chuckled.

I nodded. We said goodnight. He trundled off to bed and I headed down the hall to my room.

My body relaxed into the comfy bed but my mind wouldn't be still. Like a bad movie repeating itself, Emmett's hanging kept replaying across my tightly closed eyes. I shuddered more than once recalling how close the man had come to breathing his last breath. I should never have left him alone, knowing he was depressed. I promised myself I would take better care of Emmett in the future since God had obviously put him in my charge.

I finally drifted into a dream where I stood in a room sifting through piles of carved wooden cartoon characters like Mickey Mouse and Smokey the Bear. I heard water rushing and splashing like a brook, but I couldn't see where the water was coming from. Pieces of wooden clock parts floated around my knees. I tried to open a door but the water forced it shut. I started to panic. Solow swam into sight, dove under the water and came up with a rubber plug in his mouth. The water slurped and swirled down a drain in the middle of the floor, exposing a live alligator.

CHAPTER FOUR

It was Saturday morning, three days after the Hooley explosion and two days before I had to go back to work. I stretched and kicked off the lightweight blanket, noticing Solow was missing from his bed. Coffee aroma made its way down the hall to my bedroom. I imagined Emmett getting acquainted with Mr. Coffee and Solow hanging around the kitchen waiting for food and attention. I smiled as I pulled on my robe and shoved my feet into slippers. Having a houseguest wasn't all that bad, I thought as I dragged myself down the hall toward the scent of coffee.

"Good morning, bright eyes," David said, looking up from the newspaper.

"What...?" I ran fingers through my unruly hair, figuring I looked more like the bride of Frankenstein than not. "What are you doing here so early...? Where's Emmett?"

"Don't worry. He's taking a nap. He was busy last night and wore himself out."

I cocked my head to one side, waiting for an explanation.

"I heard something in the middle of the night. When I looked out my bedroom window, I saw Emmett with a shovel digging a hole in the ground. He was near our property line, over by the fence...the little section of fence that's still standing. The moon was huge. I saw him clear as day."

"Why would he be digging a hole in the middle of the night?"

"Well, he said he wanted to bury his wooden box before someone stole it. I asked him who would steal it but he didn't know who. I asked why they'd steal it and he said, 'because of the secret formula.'" David shrugged his shoulders. "I talked him into putting the box under his bed until we can arrange a safety deposit box at the bank."

"If it means that much to him, I suppose we should take him to the bank when we go shopping today." I yawned and took another sip of the coffee David had poured for me.

"Guess I'll go home now that you're up. I gave Solow his breakfast. Call me if you need help with anything." David opened the back door and Solow squeezed past him. With major four-legged basset propulsion, my dog took off after a certain fluffy white cat.

"I'll call you when we're ready to go shopping. Thank you, David. It was sweet of you to take care of things."

He walked outside, leaving me to deal with Emmett's quirks.

I moved quietly through the kitchen and dining room, stopped at the edge of the living room rug and watched the rise and fall of the old man's chest as he slept on the sofa. Emmett must have searched my metal shed twice, once for the rope and once for the shovel.

The phone rang. It was Alicia. We talked as I made my way to the bedroom.

"Did you just say he hung himself?"

"That's what I said. Allie, it was awful. We had to work fast…even so, we almost lost him. David was so wonderful. He knew just what to do and the paramedics were great. Now that we saved his life, Emmett wants to find the person who blew up his house. We don't know who did it and what if they have something against Emmett? I just hope they don't find out that Mr. Hooley is staying with me."

"Jo, maybe you should hand him over to the police…."

"This is going to sound strange, but I feel like he's family and I need to help him avenge his sister's murder."

"What if it was Emmett who blew up the house? You said he was in the back cottage that night. Maybe that was part of his plan."

"Allie, I know it sounds crazy, but I trust Emmett."

"I can't wait to meet the old gentleman. Why don't you stop by when you're out shopping?"

"If we have time. Thanks for the invite."

Alicia hung up and I dressed for the day. I heard the Jeep door slam and seconds later David opened the front door. We met in the hall. A pair of old rubber flip flops dangled from his two fingers and a folded Forty-niner t-shirt was tucked under one arm. After an awkward hug, he explained that Emmett was welcome to keep the shoes and shirt.

After breakfast the old man practiced walking a straight line wearing flip flops and the way-too-big red and gold t-shirt. Invariably, when he went straight the flip flops didn't. If he made a turn, they didn't. He was determined to conquer the goofy shoes or at least be able to shuffle around in them. Once he was somewhat ambulatory, the three of us piled into David's Jeep and headed east to Gilroy, the shopping Mecca of Central California.

"Emmett, do you have a favorite store you would like to go to?" David asked.

"No," came from the back seat. We were headed toward the big box stores, little box stores and a hundred zillion outlets. David and I were not big shoppers and it looked like Emmett lived in the same camp.

"I think Hilda liked that one," came from the back seat.

I cranked my head around as Emmett was pointed to a giant red bull's eye.

David made a couple right turns and parked in the closest space available, fifty yards from Target's front door. Emmett shuffled across the parking lot at an unbelievably slow speed. David and I took baby steps, trying to pace ourselves and look as if we were moving forward.

As soon as we entered the building, Emmett peeled off to the right, heading toward the restrooms. David followed him.

When the boys returned to the store entry, Emmett kept moving forward in a straight line, gliding his flip flops over to the food-court for a bag of popcorn.

David paid while I did a quick eyeball-measurement of Emmett's boney body.

"You boys enjoy the popcorn. I'll be right back." I pushed a big red shopping cart up the main aisle and turned left to the men's clothing department. According to my Aunt Clara, men are only familiar with a short list of colors, namely, light blue, denim blue, navy blue, brown and black. I decided to go crazy and buy Emmett a grey t-shirt, a white dress shirt, a black belt, jeans, and a grey hoodie. I snagged a Hawaiian shirt in multiple shades of sage green, a pair of grey slacks, grey suspenders and a set of blue and green plaid pajamas. I grabbed a couple packages of underwear from the teen-boys department and pushed my cart back to the men eating popcorn.

"That was quick," David said, as he inspected a package of boys' grey boxer shorts. "Now we need to look at shoes and socks."

Emmett straightened his back. "Yes, I would like to buy a pair of shoes."

David and I led the way to the shoe department, stopping periodically to let Mr. Hooley's flip flops catch up. Once we entered the shoe aisle, he quickly settled on a pair of black athletic shoes and a package of grey socks. David tossed a Forty-niner cap into the basket and I helped Emmett pick out a wallet.

He opened the billfold, closed it, dropped it into the basket and headed for the checkout area with David.

I joined the boys at the automatic exit door and slowly followed Emmett's flip-flop stride to the jeep, feeling thankful that Emmett was easy to please.

"Emmett, what bank do you go to?" I asked.

"The one in Watsonville…Wells Fargo."

"How about the Wells Fargo in Gilroy?" David asked.

"Watsonville," came the response.

David shrugged, pulled into Highway 101 traffic and forty minutes later he parked at the bank in Watsonville.

Emmett blinked and looked around. "Yes, this is my bank."

David helped the old man into the new socks and shoes, hoping they would speed up his pace. Unfortunately we didn't see a lot of speed as he crossed the parking lot and entered the bank, cradling his wooden box full of carving tools. David and I walked closely behind, ready to catch the old man if he stumbled in his new shoes.

Like most things in Watsonville, the bank was old, small and full of people. Emmett walked past the first two tellers, opting for the third window where a tall, stocky middle-aged woman wearing a bun on top of her head waved at him daintily.

I stayed close to Emmett in case he needed me.

"Mr. Hooley, how are you and your dear sister?" Ms. Bun smiled ear to ear.

"Hilda isn't with us any more," he said, glancing at the floor.

The woman instantly lost her smile. She politely waited for an explanation but Emmett didn't offer one. The woman looked at me and cocked her head.

"I'm with him," I said.

She took a long look at me, probably checking to see if I looked like a Hooley.

"Now, how can I help you, dear?" she asked.

"I need some money and a safe place for my...."

"...box." I said.

Ms. Bun squinted an eye at me.

I took a step back and told myself Emmett was a big boy and could take care of business.

"Mr. Hooley, follow me please," Ms. Bun said, ignoring the people lined up behind us. She snapped her fingers, ordered a young teller to take over her window and led Emmett across the room to a door on the far side of the building. They disappeared into another room leaving David and me to find a place to sit and wait. When they finally returned, the woman had black smears under her red-rimmed eyes and Emmett's wooden box was gone.

Ms. Bun took over an empty desk and Emmett sat down opposite her signing his name to several sheets of paper. She handed him a temporary checkbook. She opened a drawer, pulled out a tin box and opened it with a key. She counted out a stack of bills and then recounted them into Emmett's hands.

He folded the wad and stuffed it into his pant's pocket. He stood, she stood and they hugged.

We followed Emmett outside and across the parking lot.

"Everything taken care of?" I asked, remembering the hug at the end of business.

He nodded and climbed into the back seat.

"Get everything you wanted?" David asked, as he drove slowly across the parking lot.

"Yes I did," he said, snapping his seatbelt into position. Emmett riffled through the large Target bag full of clothes. He found the receipt and studied it for a moment as David's little Jeep entered Freedom Boulevard stop-and-go traffic.

"Josephine, can you tell me the total, please. I don't have my…."

"…glasses," I said. "The total is two-hundred and three dollars…we need to buy you a pair of glasses."

"I buy them at the drug store," he said.

David signaled for a right turn and parked in front of a Walgreens Pharmacy.

While David and Emmett explored the eyeglass displays, I found a few manly items such as a comb, razor, shaving cream, toothpaste and gargle. As I rounded the dental aisle, David smacked into me coming the other way.

"Where's Emmett?" I looked up and down the aisle.

"He wanted to sit in the Jeep. What's the matter? We found some glasses." He held up a pair for reading and a pair of sunglasses.

I shoved all the sundries into his arms and ran out the door. I quickly scanned the parking lot. Fifty feet from the store entrance Emmett was gingerly climbing into the Jeep. A dusty white van pulled in beside the Jeep and a balding man poked his head out the half-open sliding door. I took off running toward David's car telling myself I was a five-hundred pound gorilla and nobody better touch Emmett.

The man in the van turned his head when he heard the pounding of my shoes. He ducked back inside and the door closed.

I quickly climbed into the passenger seat of the Jeep, locked the doors and waited for David. I was still breathing hard when he arrived.

"What's going on, Josie? Your face is red."

"Probably just my imagination," I mumbled. I buckled up for the ride home, noticing that the white van was gone. "Dang! I forgot to get the license, I mean...ah, the newspaper. I forgot to...ah bring in the paper this morning."

David looked at me and smiled. "The paper is in your kitchen, sweetie." He scratched his head of thick salt and pepper hair, started the jeep and turned right onto Freedom Boulevard.

I spotted the van one block and twenty cars ahead of us.

"Hurry, David, follow that van," I shouted, pointing to the white vehicle at the head of the pack, waiting for a light to change.

David frowned. "Really, we need to follow that...."

The light turned green and the van took off. We had no chance of catching up. I covered my face with my hands.

"Honey, what's going on?"

"Nothing." I ripped the tags off Emmett's sunglasses. "Here, Emmett, you can wear your new glasses now." The image of Einstein in sunglasses and a forty-niner shirt made me smile. "I'm sorry, David, I thought Emmett was in danger...forget it." David turned his head my way.

"What made you think he was in...."

"...danger?" Emmett added.

I realized at that moment the old man was fully capable of understanding his own predicament.

David's noisy Jeep jolted forward and entered the flow of traffic.

"Emmett, did you see the man in the white van?" I asked.

"As a matter of fact, I did. It was Arnie. He works as a security guard at the bank. He was stationed in the back room by the safe today."

"So, you're saying he works at the Wells Fargo Bank we went to today?"

"Yes. His name is Arnie Harburg. His mother was a friend of my sister. She and Hilda played Skat every Thursday with a group of ladies at the German Hall. I was in the men's group and we played chess."

"What is Skat?" I asked, as a picture of animal droppings buzzed through my mind.

"It's a three-handed card game. Sometimes they played Tarock or Schafkopf."

"But you always played Chess? Did Arnie play...."

"...Chess? No, he has to work. He supports his mother and I think they're rather poor."

"How about the lady at the bank with the bun on her head, do you know her?"

"I know Gertrude. She was married to my cousin's son, Ed, and she handles all my accounts." Emmett dropped his head back against the seat and closed his eyes, a signal to me to cut the chatter.

David gently squeezed my hand, his way of saying, "Give Emmett a break."

My problem was I didn't believe in coincidences. Why was Arnie parked beside David's Jeep just minutes after the bank transactions? Eventually my mind wandered over to the fact that I was starving hungry and Alicia's house was only five minutes away. I conveyed that message to our handsome driver and soon we were rolling through the Lake District.

Emmett heard the engine shut down and opened his eyes.

"Where are we?"

"This is where our friends, the Quintanas, live." David said, holding the door open for the old man. "They're anxious to meet you."

"Allie always asks about you," I added.

Trigger pounded down the stairs when he heard the doorbell. He flung open the door and hugged me.

Emmett smiled the biggest smile I'd seen so far when Trigger shook his hand and led him into the living room.

Alicia and Ernie left their empty plates at the breakfast bar and joined us with smiles and hugs.

"We wondered if you were coming," Alicia said. "We just finished our lunch but I'll rustle up some more sandwiches."

I followed her back to the kitchen where I watched her make three more sandwiches while the boys relaxed in the living room.

"Emmett looks good for his age," Alicia commented.

"Yeah, not as bad as the first couple days. We bought him some new clothes today. He doesn't act depressed any more, just a little tired. He's been through a lot. I handed him his mail and he just put it in the glove compartment—wouldn't deal with it. In fact, it's still there." I made a mental note to bring his mail into the house at the first opportunity.

"It must be awful for Emmett to lose his sister. I have two sisters...." Alicia's voice trailed off to a whisper.

"I didn't know you had sisters. You had to leave them behind when you were adopted?"

Alicia nodded.

"Have you seen or heard from either of them over the years?" Alicia had already told me about living in Tijuana, selling chewing gum on the streets at six years old and then her adoption by a middle-aged American couple, but she'd never mentioned her family in Mexico.

"No, I've never heard from my sisters. They were a little older and probably stayed on the streets of Tijuana. I like to think that good things happened to them, but I'll never know. I don't even know how to find them."

"I know one way," I said. "Give your sisters' names to Trigger and let him explore the internet."

"He is good...better than I'll ever be on a computer," she said as we carried the food to the table.

David, Emmett and I began eating our sandwiches. Trigger served himself a scoop of ice cream and his parents sipped iced tea. Through the dining room windows we had a first class view of glistening lake water lapping against the Quintana lawn. A lone canoe sliced a path through the deep blue water while ducks, geese and coots scattered toward the opposite shore.

"What lake am I looking at?" Emmett asked.

"Drew Lake," Ernie said. "Watch those crazy geese. They think they're ducks." We all turned in our chairs to watch a swarm of ducks skimming across the lake with two grey geese bringing up the rear. "Would you like to go fishing after you eat?"

Emmett's face lit up like a sunrise.

"Oh my, I haven't fished since I was a boy," he chuckled, patting his whiskery face with a paper napkin. He didn't need a second invitation.

When the dishes were clean and the lake had been fished by two men in a peddle-boat, we thanked the Quintanas and headed home.

As David's Jeep bounced along the highway, Emmett held on to his big-eyed fish wrapped in newspaper. The fish was small but he wanted to give it to Fluffy. He had tried to throw the little bass back into the lake but his arm became tangled in the fishing line. By the time Ernie unscrambled him, Mr. Fish was dead.

"Emmett...oh, sorry, thought you were awake."

He looked around. "Yes, Josephine, what can I do for you?"

"I was just thinking I might take a shower when we get home, how about you? You can go first if you like."

"Are you suggesting a shower because I smell like fish and lake water?" he laughed. "My pants and shoes are still wet. I hope the shoes can be washed."

"No problem," I said. "I hate to say it, but that was the funniest thing I ever saw. That old goose must have thought you were the Lochness Monster the way he flapped his wings and hissed at you. He chased the boat for at least ten minutes. Did you see Trigger yelling and pointing? Allie and I laughed until our sides hurt. I hope the goose didn't hurt you."

"No, he didn't hurt me. It was perplexing all right."

CHAPTER FIVE

I woke up startled by the realization that it was already Sunday, one day before my big mural job was scheduled to begin. Even with Alicia and Kyle's help, it seemed like a daunting project. I couldn't decide whether my heart palpitations were worry or excitement. Either way I needed to prepare, go over the sketches and organize the paints and supplies.

I'd already called Kyle. He sounded more than happy to have a paying job, mentioning that his rent was due. Lucky for me, the young UCSC student was a genius when it came to wielding a paint brush.

My painting company, Wildbrush Murals, had a contract with members of the Halikias family to paint a mural on the outside wall of a new art gallery in Moss Landing. The converted sardine factory was the last packing house in a row of about twenty renovated buildings. They all faced the Moss Landing Harbor, an ideal home for commercial fishing boats and renovated packing sheds. The buildings were backed up to the slough, a natural buffer between the Pacific Ocean and the little harbor.

Because it was my last day off for awhile, I told myself to relax—enjoy the moment. I set my new job worries aside, closed my eyes and let my mind bounce around to various thoughts and memories. I laughed to myself when I remembered Ernie and Emmett's fishing trip the day before. No matter how fast the men peddled—that old goose was right there skittering across the water, flapping his wings and honking. Emmett had kept his composure under fire. If that goose had attacked me, I think I'd have freaked out and smacked him with the bait box.

When I finally opened my eyes and looked around the room, I noticed Solow wasn't in his bed. I rolled out of mine, slipped on a robe and followed the coffee scent to the kitchen.

"Good morning, Miss Josephine." Emmett pretended to tip a non-existent hat.

"Emmett, I hardly know you—all shaved and wearing clothes that fit. Looks like you're growing a mustache. Nice. How about a haircut today?"

"That would be very nice. Hilda always cut my hair."

"Maybe we should darken your hair...kind of a disguise in case someone is looking for you."

He quickly nodded his OK.

After breakfast, I gathered up scissors, comb and razor. Emmett sat motionless wrapped in a beach towel on a chair placed in the center of the back patio. I repeatedly combed and snipped until only half an inch of white fluff remained. His head had shrunk by half.

Even as we worked on changing Emmett's "look," I was discovering who he was at heart. We talked about his family, my family and issues of the day. He was smart and funny, he had friends, he had hobbies, he had a full life before Hilda and the house blew up. I shook tons of white hair off the towel and we went inside.

"Nice sideburns," he said, looking in the mirror I handed him. "I look like an old Jewish country western singer," he snickered.

There was a tap, tap at the back door. It opened and David walked in.

"Holy moly—what a difference a haircut makes!" He slapped his forehead with the palm of his hand for affect. "Nice work, Josephine."

"How do you know I did it?"

"The sideburns are uneven."

"I knew that. Don't worry, Emmett, I'll even them up. By the way, David, do you still have the hair dye…?

"The dye you said you didn't like because you like my greying hair?" He smiled and smoothed a patch of hair with his hand.

"Yeah, that comb-in stuff. We're giving Emmett a new look." I winked.

"He looks pretty new already. Thought he was a rock star at first glance."

Emmett laughed, sending Solow into an extended howl.

"I came by to see if you two would like to take a walk up the road—check out Emmett's place when the deputies aren't there."

Emmett raised his bushy eyebrows. "A walk would be nice. I've been worried about Lilly and my cabbage plants."

He named a cabbage plant, Lilly? I didn't understand naming plants since mine were lucky to get a ration of water now and then.

"I can't stay too long…gotta work on the mural details later this afternoon," I said, thinking out loud. I had already researched Greek architecture and drawn several sketches. The owners of Halikias Gallery, Irene and her brother, Nico Halikias, liked my sketches of a Greek temple. Irene said she wanted the Parthenon, but not all crumbly. I said I could do that. But could I?

David and I gave Emmett and Solow a little head start but caught up to them at the end of my long gravel driveway. It was good to see the old man chugging along, breathing fresh air and exercising his legs. Solow stayed right by his side, causing me to suffer pangs of jealousy.

David held my hand as we slowly strolled up Otis Road and then Emmett's driveway.

Emmett kept walking—didn't even turn his head toward his cindered home. He huffed and puffed up the hill and spread his arms wide. Suddenly he was hugging a goat.

I blinked. Yep, it was a little brown goat with white socks and muzzle.

David laughed. "He's hugging a goat!"

"Yeah...must be his?" I couldn't take my eyes off the sweet man-goat reunion. We caught up to Emmett who had a grip on the goat's lavender collar. "A friend of yours?"

"This is Lilly. She's an eight-month-old Toggenburg nanny. Her job is to keep the weeds down." He grinned as Lilly nuzzled his pockets. "She wants a treat but my pockets are empty," he sighed.

Solow had finally caught up to us. He circled the goat twice, sniffing the ground as he went.

"Emmett, do these two know each other?" David asked.

"Yes they do, and they both want the same thing...treats." He gave Lilly a pat on the rear and the little goat galloped up the hill toward a string of eucalyptus. "She's never been fenced in. She's too much of a free spirit."

"What about wild animals?" I asked, as Emmett turned on a tap and filled a bucket with water from the hose.

"Except for a cougar, she can protect herself with her little horns and sharp hooves. She used to sleep under the porch at night. I'm wondering where she sleeps now." Emmett stroked his new mustache. "She's a very smart nanny. We had to put up a wire fence around the vegetable garden and you'll notice the fruit trees don't have leaves or branches down low. Lilly can spot a liverwurst sandwich at thirty yards," he laughed.

"Are you planning to bring her back to my house?" In my mind Lilly was romping through my house, surfing the counters for food and devouring my books.

"No, no need to do that. I taught Lilly to stay on my property...she's my little pet."

We moved slowly up the hill to the ring of foliage, entered the inner garden circle and then the cottage. David's jaw dropped when he saw the carved figures strewn across the room. He crouched down and ran his fingers over an especially beautiful carved and painted peasant woman wearing a long blue skirt, white apron and shawl.

I found an empty plastic bucket and we began filling it with wooden figures.

An hour later we had a full bucket and two grocery bags full of cuckoo parts.

Emmett filled an old metal lunch box with clock innards and tools he carefully rescued from the debris.

"Looks like you'll be busy, Emmett, while I'm at work tomorrow."

"Yes, I need to be busy." He carried the lunch box to my house and stashed it in the loft. The boys settled down to popcorn and a movie while I scrounged around in the back shed gathering all sorts of mural-making tools. I loaded my truck with ladders, tarps, tape, toolbox and several gallons and many quarts of acrylic paint. I tossed in three two-foot levels and a box of colored chalk.

I pulled the Mazda's metal bed-top down until it rested on my eight-foot ladder. Two feet of the ladder poked out over the tailgate.

The Halikias' mural wall was thirty-five feet wide by fifteen feet high. Upon my advice, the owners of the gallery had the original wooden wall covered with a smooth coat of plaster and pale blue paint. I'd inspected the building the day before Emmett's house blew up. Since then it had been hard to concentrate on the project. Other than keeping Mr. Hooley safe and finding Hilda's murderer, all I had to do was paint a giant Greek temple. What could possibly go wrong?

When my truck was finally loaded, I dragged myself back into the house to look for something to eat.

"What's that heavenly smell, David? Are you baking something?"

"Just keeping it warm until you're ready to eat," he said, heading for the kitchen.

"What is it?"

"Fettuccini Florentina with basil walnut pesto."

"Oh, that sounds scrumptious." Envious of his culinary skills, but salivating at the thought of yummy Italian food, I sat down at the dining room table next to Emmett and made sure the old man had plenty of pasta and salad.

Emmett ate like a man who hadn't eaten in several days. It was the first time I'd seen him eat and smile at the same time.

It was eight o'clock and we'd barely finished our mocha mousse desserts when there was a sharp knock on the front door.

Solow galloped to the front door, his growls turning into sharp, excited barks.

I followed him with a spoon in one hand and a napkin in the other. I swallowed my last luscious bite of mousse and shouted at the door.

"Come in."

The muffled voices coming from the front porch stopped and the door slowly opened. Solow squeezed past me and greeted Deputy Sayer.

Deputy Lund didn't look happy, but that was nothing new.

"We need to talk to Mr. Hooley," she said, eyeing the boys at the table. She whipped her head around a second time in Emmett's direction.

Like her, I still found it hard to believe he was the same gentleman as the disheveled barefoot old man I met four days earlier.

"Come in and sit down," I said in my most gracious voice.

The deputies sat down on the sofa and Emmett sat in the old wing chair with Solow at his feet.

David excused himself and disappeared out the front door. We heard the Jeep fire up.

I sat down in the rocking chair.

Deputy Sayer fiddled with a file folder he held in his lap.

"Mr. Hooley, a preliminary report has been filed and we came here tonight to explain it to you. Ms. Stuart, since you are the caregiver...."

"I'm not a caregiver. Does Mr. Hooley look like he needs care?" I snapped. How dare Sayer degrade my friend like that. All Emmett needed was some clothes, shoes and a haircut to look like a million bucks. The hair dye had knocked his age down at least ten years.

"I meant to say," Deputy Sayer started over, "since he's living with you, Josephine, I will tell both of you what we know so far." He opened the folder and ran his eyes down the top page. "We have conclusive proof that Hilda Hooley died in the fire. Her dentist has made a positive identification."

I turned and looked at Emmett who sat staring at Solow's broad backside.

"How did it happen?" I asked.

"He's getting to that, Ms. Stuart," Deputy Lund said.

Sayer continued. "The arson investigator is pretty sure that a stove or furnace was leaking propane...."

"We had no gas leaks," Emmett said, matter-of-factly.

Sayer checked his paperwork.

"Somehow gas was leaking. Maybe a stove was left on. No one knows for sure."

"We never left the gas on without flame. Why would we do that?" Emmet asked.

I had my own burning questions and plenty of them. "Officer Sayer, wouldn't there have to be a spark of some kind? Do you know what sparked the explosion?"

"It says here that the spark is unknown at this point in the investigation." He glanced at the sheet of paper and then raised his eyes back to Emmett. "Your sister died in her bed."

"Did someone break into the house?" I asked.

Lund shook her head. "The investigator was able to determine that the back door was not locked...."

"The door was not locked," Emmet took a long breath, "because I was working in the cottage. Hilda went back to the house around ten. I decided to work a little longer. I remember feeling tired so I took a nap on the cot. The next thing I knew there was a big noise and I was thrown to the floor."

"Mr. Hooley, what did you do then?" Sayer asked.

"When I fell, I hit my head on something and I had a hard time standing up. Finally I was able to walk outside. I looked up at the flames all over my beautiful house…then I remembered Hilda was inside. There were flames all over the roof and smoke everywhere. As I got closer to the fire, someone ran into me and knocked me down." Emmett pulled up his pant leg and showed us a massive purple-going-yellow bruise on the side of his knee.

My jaw went slack and even Deputy Lund's eyes softened for a moment.

Deputy Sayer tried hard to stick to business.

"Mr. Hooley, did you see who knocked you down?"

"No, it was dark."

"Do you have any idea who it could have been?"

"No, but my tooth fell out."

"Mr. Hooley, did you keep any valuables in your wall-safe?" Deputy Lund asked.

"Why?"

"Just answer the question, please."

"The answer is, no," Emmett said, studying his new shoes.

Sayer checked the report. "It says here the fire inspector found an empty safe. The door was open, but since you say you had nothing in it, you obviously were not robbed."

I squirmed in my rocker. "Just because nothing was taken from the safe doesn't mean there wasn't a robbery," I said, kicking my rocker into a higher speed.

"Mr. Hooley, does anyone know that you're living in this house with Ms. Stuart?" Deputy Lund asked.

I answered the question before Emmett could open his mouth. "We don't advertise the fact. Only my two best friends and my parents know." Heat flooded my cheeks as I realized one of those confidants might accidentally tell someone else. "Besides, we're working on a disguise for Mr. Hooley."

Lund eyed him all the way down to his new black athletic shoes. "You can try but I don't think you can hide his very, ah, distinctive characteristics." Officer Lund glanced at Sayer for back up but the deputy kept his head down thumbing through the report.

Finally he spoke. "Mr. Hooley, you are mentioned in the report as a 'person of interest.' Do you understand what that means, Sir?"

"Yes I do understand, but you should not waste time on me when a killer is running free."

I nodded my head enthusiastically.

The officers stood and walked to the door.

"If any suspicious persons come to your house, call 911 immediately," Sayer said, "and don't leave town."

As the officers walked to their cruiser, I wondered if they thought Emmett was guilty.

The phone rang. I snagged it.

Mom's voice rose as she told me about her day, how she and Dad had spent hours planting a little vegetable garden in their back yard. When they finished planting they went in the house for a cup of tea, unaware that the neighbor's six-month-old black lab was digging a hole under the fence. It seems he ran circles through the delicate new plants, grinding them into obscurity.

"Wow, that's too bad about Dad's garden. How did he take it?"

"Like a man. He kicked the barbeque. He's soaking his toe as we speak."

"Mom, remember I told you about Mr. Hooley? His house burned down and his sister died? Well, the Sheriff's deputies were just here and reminded me that we can't tell anyone Emmett is living here...OK?"

"You mean because of what people would think…?"

"No, no, Mom, because there might be a…ah, sort of mean person trying to find him."

"What you're saying is, there's a murderer looking for him," she gasped.

"You could say that." I cringed. "But don't worry. David is right next door and Solow barks if anyone comes to my door. I met Emmett's goat today."

"Honey, don't try to change the subject…the man has a goat?"

"Hey, we live in Aromas. Lots of people have them. Lilly is a beautiful brown nanny goat with a white face and stockings. She might still be a kid—she's only eight months old. Emmett trained her to do all kinds of things and Solow gets along with her."

"I won't tell a soul about Emmett living in your house, dear. Of course I had to tell Myrtle, but I'll tell her to keep it to herself." She paused, probably trying to think of other people she told. I rolled my eyes to the ceiling and asked God to watch over us. I had a hunch we'd need help.

CHAPTER SIX

I automatically hit the snooze button and instantly realized there would be no snooze. It was seven o'clock Monday morning, time to get up and ready to go to work. I rolled out of bed, tippy-toed past Solow and made a left into the hall. The bathroom door was closed and I heard running water. I decided to bypass the bathroom and put Mr. Coffee to work instead.

As I entered the kitchen, I heard footsteps behind me.

"Good morning, Miss Josephine," Emmett said, smiling ear-to-ear.

"Good morning. Don't you look spiffy today? What have you been up to?"

"I had a refreshing shower after my walk to the house," he smiled.

"Emmett, you can't, I mean you can not...go wandering around this neighborhood alone!" My jaw was clenched and my eyes would have been shooting sparks if I could have conjured up some. Emmett's eyes focused on the floor, forcing me to bring it down a couple notches. "Somebody is after you. If you need to go to your house, David or I will take you...OK?" I marched down the hall to my room and slipped into a freshly laundered but paint-stained t-shirt, old jeans and sandals.

I hurried back to the kitchen and began making breakfast, hoping to soothe the poor man with my home cooking. I could have boiled goose droppings and snail shells and he would have thanked me for the delicious meal. His mother had raised a real gentleman.

After breakfast, I loaded a few last minute paint supplies into the truck and gave Emmett a long look that said, "Don't you dare wander this neighborhood!"

He gave me a, "Yes, Ma'am" salute.

Solow didn't even follow me to the door. After all, he had Emmett all to himself.

I began my commute thinking about the mural I'd promised to paint. Irene and Nico had fulfilled their part of the mural preparation by having the wall plastered and painted. Now it was up to me and my cohorts to paint a subject we'd never attempted before. In my mind I pictured the Greek temple rising up to within two feet of the flat-roof, leaving a section of blue along the top to blend with the California sky.

As I drove southwest on Highway One, I painted a Greek temple in my mind. I measured, cut out templates, mixed up five shades of off-white paint, applied a watered-down purple where shadows were needed, highlighted sections of the columns and architectural features with pure white and signed my name at the bottom—along with Alicia and Kyle. I was ready to run through the process again when I realized I was just two pelicans short of Moss Landing. The morning fog had thickened and gulls darted in and out of view like ghosts.

I left the highway, following a narrow curvy road into town. As I motored over a short bridge, I looked down at the harbor crammed with commercial fishing boats. I continued on the road, passing by a string of renovated cannery buildings, better known as down town Moss Landing.

The Halikias Gallery sat on a rise at the end of the street, just eight feet above sea level and surrounded by water on three sides. It would be the last building to get a face-lift, probably the most dramatic change of all the buildings in town.

I parked in the slot nearest the front door and began unloading equipment.

The roar of a motorcycle caught my attention.

"Hi, Kyle. You arrived just in time," I shouted.

Kyle slid his yellow Honda into the space next to mine and cut the engine.

He pulled off his helmet, unsnapped his chaps and ran fingers through spiky red hair. He asked about Alicia.

"She'll be here...oh, here she is now." Alicia parked her green Volvo station wagon and hurried over to help empty my truck. Her black shoulder-length hair shone, her smile was radiant and her jeans and t-shirt had no paint stains on them. Alicia was a hard-working artist, but at the end of the day she always looked fresh and clean as if she'd just come from the spa. I guess she never learned to use her shirt as a hand towel.

Kyle grabbed the eight-foot ladder, Alicia hooked an arm around the six-footer and I picked up the three-footer. They were younger and usually did the heavier lifting. We unloaded several gallons and many quarts of paint, canvas bags full of supplies, tarps and levels, not to mention a very heavy tackle box loaded with bottles of paint.

Irene and Nico, looking fit and thirtyish, stepped outside wearing big smiles. They were brother and sister and obviously close in age. As soon as I introduced everyone, Nico went back inside and Irene led us to the left side of the building where a long narrow tin shed filled the space between the gallery and the kayak rental shop next door.

"This is where you can keep your equipment at night...OK?

"OK, it's perfect," I said. "Irene, do you think the fog will lift?"

"Oh sure." She checked her watch. "Give it half an hour."

Sure enough, half an hour later the sun broke through and stayed with us until three. By that time, we'd measured and drawn the entire Greek temple on the wall.

Kyle taped around the frame of the gallery's double-door entrance which happened to be perfectly suited to look like an entrance to the Parthenon.

Alicia and I mixed up five shades of off-white in quart-size buckets—the darkest being a faded Payne's grey-beige. Because Moss Landing spent half its life in the fog, I added a tinge of warm yellow to the three lightest shades.

Wisps of moist air began collecting overhead, bringing a chill to my bones.

From time to time, pedestrians strolled out to the gallery to see what was going on. There wasn't much to look at, just three painters representing three different generations working on a pale blue wall. By the time we left for home, everything had been measured, drawn and taped and special colors of paint were mixed.

The fog thickened into pea soup. A deep-throated horn sounded in the distance.

I drove through Moss Landing to Highway One, turned south into heavy commuter traffic, made a u-turn half a mile down the road and motored north to Watsonville.

I decided to stop at the grocery store, parked the truck, entered the market and found Robert working the frozen food aisle.

"Josephine, how's the painting going?"

"What makes you think I was painting?"

Robert eyed me up and down and shrugged.

"If that isn't paint, I guess you must have lost the food fight."

"Actually, this paint is from past murals. We didn't dribble or splash. The actual painting starts tomorrow."

Robert stocked the last of the frozen pies and then removed his gloves.

"I heard something about your neighbor today."

"What neighbor?" I asked.

"Howdy, Hoody, Wally...."

"Oh, you mean Mr. Hooley. What about him?"

"KPIG news said Mr. Hooley's sister died in that fire and the police are looking for an arsonist."

"Did they say anything else? Was there a description of the guy?"

Robert shook his head and pushed an empty dolly toward the back of the store.

I loaded my basket with fresh produce, meat and a loaf of rye bread. I topped it all off with a dozen eggs, ice cream and toilet paper. Half my mind was on shopping—the other half was wondering why an arsonist would go all the way to Aromas to burn something down.

I rounded a corner and stopped short when I saw a middle-aged couple ahead of me. I recognized the bun on the top of the plump lady's head and the shiny bald spot on the guy next to her. The man wore a blue uniform that would have looked good on a smaller, younger guy. Gertrude and Arnie sauntered up the aisle just ten feet ahead of me. Gertrude stopped, gathered half a dozen cans of cat food and dropped them into the hand basket Arnie carried.

I turned away, inspecting the various brands of dog food.

They moved on and I followed at a distance. They talked to each other, but I couldn't make out the words. On the next aisle, they stopped to pick out a bottle of salad dressing.

I turned to my right to inspect pickles.

"Oops!" popped out of my mouth as a slippery bottle of kosher dills hit the floor sending pickles, glass and juice six feet in every direction. I glanced at the couple.

They gawked for a moment then walked away.

"Jo!" Robert caught up to me.

I twirled around, heart pounding.

"What happened, Jo?"

"Oh, I was just speculating…about something, and the bottle slipped out of my hand. I didn't hear you coming. Sorry about the mess."

"I didn't mean to scare you." He ignored the mess as he held out two baskets of fresh strawberries for my inspection. "I know how much you like strawberries and I just wanted to let you know that they're good and sweet today, and the price isn't bad."

"Great. I'll take two baskets."

Robert placed the strawberries on top of the egg carton and pulled my cart into his checking lane. On tip-toes he leaned into his microphone and called for a clean-up on aisle four. He rang up my items, but he stopped his bagging to watch me as I watched Gertrude and Arnie leave the store with one bag of groceries.

"You know them?" he asked.

"Not really. Do you?"

"Arnie works security here once a year when we have our big parking lot sale. He tries to look tough with that pepper spray hooked on his belt."

Robert lifted the heavy bags into my cart and walked me to my truck.

"Are you sure you don't know them?" he asked.

"I don't know them personally. Do you know the woman?"

Robert shook his head, turned and said goodbye.

I wondered if the boy had a "life" other than his devotion to the market. I jumped in the truck and concentrated on stop-and-go commuter traffic. I quickly changed lanes, ignored the honking and veered right, heading for the Pajaro River. I cruised up to the top of the five lane bridge and started down the other side.

Like an unexpected nightmare, an ancient pock-marked maroon Oldsmobile ran a light and broadsided the Ford pickup I was following.

I slammed on the brakes, dropping the speed from twenty to zero in a split second. My heart pounded and my legs went wobbly. I'd been spared by two seconds. It could have been me with an air bag stuck to my face. I heard sirens coming from behind and saw a highway patrol car moving through traffic in my direction, lights and siren engaged. I gulped some air and thanked God that no one had been killed. However, the old man in the truck was taken away in an ambulance.

Traffic was static in four directions. Time dragged as I waited for the vehicles involved to be towed away so that the police could finish investigating and cleaning the intersection. I hoped someone would ask me who was at fault since I saw the Honda run a red light and smash into the innocent little pickup truck. I dusted my dash with a Kleenex, organized my purse and opened the glove box to straighten it. I noticed Emmett's mail tightly wedged between tennis balls and a petrified burger from last November when I was running late and didn't have time to eat before my mammogram appointment. After the appointment, I wasn't hungry.

I managed to extract the envelopes and slammed the little door before anything fell out. I told myself not to be too curious—right! I compromised by not actually opening anything. I simply sorted the forgotten mail and made a list of return addresses.

I had barely finished the list when a face appeared in my half-open driver's-side window.

"Ma'am, you can move along now," the officer said.

"But don't you want to know what I saw...?"

He left me with my mouth hanging open. "Fine!" I started the engine, cautiously rolled across the intersection and headed up San Juan Road. My quivering legs regained their strength as I imagined myself tattling on the Honda guy. From that thought, my mind skipped over to Emmett's mail, specifically a set of airline tickets. I was dying to know where and when he was going, and would he go out of town after the deputies last words, "...and don't leave town."

I drove up my driveway and parked in the usual spot near the front door. If I lived anywhere else there would have been a lawn separating the vehicle from the house, but it was casual, unpretentious Aromas. Most of my neighbors loved country life. They raised a lamb or a goat to keep the weeds down and planted vegetables in the spring. Every summer I wished I'd planted a few tomato plants, but it was too late—again.

The front door opened and Emmett peeked out.

I stuffed Emmet's mail into my purse, hooked the purse over my shoulder and climbed out of the pickup. I gathered up two bags of groceries and made my way to the front door.

Solow met me with lots of whining and tail wagging, more enthusiasm than I'd seen in a long time. I was enjoying all the fuss when suddenly something nudged me from behind. I whirled around, coming face-to-face with Lilly. I laughed nervously as she gave me another gentle butt with her head.

"Hold it, Lilly!" I said as I stepped into the living room, and Emmett quickly closed the door behind me.

He tried to suppress a smile. "Josephine, how was your day at work?"

"It went really well," I said as I unloaded one of the bags. "The ride home wasn't so great. This crazy foreign-looking woman drove her car through a red light and hit the truck in front of me. It could have been me. Guess it's my lucky day. How was your day, Mr. Hooley?"

"You don't need to call me Mister. Some of my friends just call me Hooley. Do you need help with the groceries?"

"Ah, sure, that would be nice. There's one more bag in the passenger seat."

Emmett stepped outside. Moments later there was a crash followed by strong manly words.

I ran to the front door and flung it open.

Mr. Hooley sat on the ground near the front porch, surrounded by food and a torn grocery sack. He shouted and waved at Lilly as she snatched an apple, devoured it and then began slurping ice cream from an open container.

Solow squeezed by me and helped himself to the accidental banquet.

I laughed so hard I could hardly hold onto Emmett's arm as I helped him to his feet.

He wasn't laughing. "I'm truly sorry, Josephine. I'm afraid Lilly has not adjusted well to the living arrangement."

"Can you teach her to mow my yard? I wouldn't mind having her around as long as we keep the groceries away from her." We watched Lilly and Solow lap up ice cream, already melted due to the "nasty Oldsmobile delay."

"I could clear a space in the shed. Do goats worry about spiders?"

"Not that I'm aware of," he said. "Lilly wouldn't need much room, just a place to sleep at night, and she will definitely eat your grass. I don't need to teach her." Emmett was smiling as we gathered up four packages of meat, a bag of smashed strawberries and a disfigured loaf of rye bread. I knew Lilly and Solow would clean up the rest.

Once the groceries were put away, I scanned the fridge for dinner material.

"Josephine, may I buy a dinner for you?" Emmett asked. "You look tired."

"That would be wonderful, Hooley. What did you have in mind?"

"The market in Aromas sells burritos." He had a crooked smile and his eyes twinkled. "I have tasted them a couple times with my friend. Hilda didn't believe we should spend money on prepared food."

"They make good burritos, but have you tasted the tamales?" I asked.

Emmett shook his head. "I would be very willing to try a tamale," he grinned.

"I'll drive you down there, but first, I have your mail."

I pulled seven envelopes and one postcard from my purse and handed them to Mr. Hooley. He sat down at the kitchen table and sorted through the pile. He went back to the postcard and then to an envelope with only a dirty fingerprint for a return address. He stared at the smudgy print but didn't open anything. Without a word, he stood up and carried the mail to his room.

Setting aside my raging curiosity, I went to my room and exchanged paint clothes for a clean blouse and slacks and ran a brush through my hair. I called Solow into the house, fed him his ration of kibble and called Emmett.

The old man walked to the stair rail and looked down. The twinkle was gone from his eyes.

"I'm sorry, Josephine. You go ahead—I'm not hungry."

I suddenly had a flashback of Emmett hanging from the railing. I squeezed my eyes shut for several seconds hoping to escape the horrible image. There was no way I would leave the house without him.

CHAPTER SEVEN

It was seven o'clock Tuesday morning and something didn't feel right. The alarm went off at the designated time, the sun bubbled up from the eastern hills and the birds sang every annoying song they knew. But something didn't feel right. I yawned, remembering the night before, the boring leftovers for dinner, the lack of conversation on Emmett's part and my burning desire to know more about his mail. I had had to endure all that without David because he was at his lodge meeting.

I showered and dressed for work. When I finally reached the kitchen, there was no perked coffee, no Solow and no Mr. Hooley. I checked the rest of the house and found the old man asleep on the couch with Solow close by. I tippy-toed out the door, climbed into the truck and drove to the Aromas Market for a burrito breakfast and coffee. I sat at a picnic table outside the market, pouring over the list of Emmett's mail I had jotted down on the back of an old receipt the day before. First, I studied the one and only line hand-printed on the postcard.

"I'm coming for a visit," signed, "Rose" and no return address. I remembered the glossy picture side of the card featuring a close-up shot of a white begonia. The card reminded me of the time David took me to the Begonia Festival in Capitola. It was September, the fog had cleared from the coast and parking was impossible in the village. We parked six blocks from the ocean and followed the flow of slow-moving flip flops to the main event.

We stood at the edge of Soquel Creek watching dozens of boats and make-shift floating devices gliding gracefully down the river, each one decorated to the hilt in freshly picked begonias. People and dogs swam alongside the floats all the way to the end of the line, which was a man-made pond, created by bulldozing sand into a half-circle levy. A long stretch of Capitola beach rose above and between river and ocean.

I popped the last bite of burrito into my mouth, tossed my trash in the garbage and climbed into the truck. Worries about Emmett's mood dogged me all the way to the coast where a mountain of fog had swallowed up everything in Moss Landing, including Alicia and Kyle. From a distance, my painters looked like shadows pulling paint supplies and ladders from the tin shed.

I joined my friends, adding my share of muscle to the project.

"Good Morning, Jo," Alicia said. "How was the drive home yesterday?"

"You heard about the accident?"

She nodded. "You and your truck were on the front page of the Sentinel this morning."

"It happened right in front of me. This crazy Honda sailed through a red light and bam! Just lucky no one was killed."

"What did you do, Jo?" Kyle asked.

"I was locked in…nothing I could do but wait about twenty minutes for the cops to clean it up and write their report. Can you believe how thick this fog is? I hope it clears soon. I'm afraid our paint might run." I pulled the legs apart on a six-foot ladder and pushed it into position, Kyle moved the eight-footer close to the wall and Alicia spread tarps over a long row of rosemary bushes growing between the building and the sidewalk.

"We'll start with this darker cream color...here's the sketch." I opened the folder and laid it on top of a gallon of white paint. "We cover these areas, working around the columns, and later lay in some shadows. After that, we paint the pillars, shade the left sides and highlight the right sides. The carved figures at the top will be last...just remember, the light is coming from the east. Kyle, you're the youngest. You take the eight-footer and work left to right across the top of the building. Allie, you get the six-footer and you start on the far right, halfway up. I'll take the lower third since I'm older."

"It's about time you admitted it, Jo," Allie laughed.

Kyle was already halfway up his ladder. He looked down.

"Josephine, I think you paint very well for an older person."

I flinched. "Thanks a lot, Kyle."

After about ten minutes of intense painting, a white van with Arizona plates pulled into the handicapped parking space next to my truck. A heavy-set woman wearing a dirty-blond ponytail, skimpy summer clothes and heavy-duty work boots climbed down from the driver's seat. She wrapped her arms around her love-handles and shivered.

"Hi, need some help?" I asked as she marched toward the double doors. "The Halikias' aren't here yet."

She looked up at the three nonsensical patches of new paint we'd just applied and smirked. She tried the entry doors, gave up and climbed back into the van.

Moments later, Irene and Nico pulled up in their late model black Mercedes. Nico went straight to the van to talk to the driver and Irene unlocked the entrance doors. Nico walked the unfriendly woman to the door.

"How many paintings?" he asked her.

I couldn't hear her answer, but a little later I watched the woman unload half a dozen four-foot by six-foot framed oil paintings from the back of the van. Nico helped her carry them into the building. The dark colored splashes and dribbles of paint reminded me of what happens when caffeinated chimpanzees get a hold of paint and brushes.

I silently scolded myself for being overly critical.

The woman climbed into the van and drove away, as the sun broke through multi-layers of wispy fog.

Our employers came outside to say, hello.

"Looks like you're already filling the gallery," I said.

"Roy paints and Kat delivers," Irene said, squinting into the sun. "The grand opening is three weeks away and there's so much to do."

"OK, Nico, let's get back to work." The Halikias went back inside.

I pushed on a pair of sunglasses, shed my hoodie and traded shoes for flip flops. It was going to be a warm day with no shade until five o'clock quitting time. On the upside, we were surrounded on three sides by lapping seawater, chugging trawlers, screeching gulls and barking sea lions. And two fantastic fish restaurants in easy walking distance.

By noon we were ready to relax. Kyle suggested a fish and chips place three doors down from the gallery.

"OK, Kyle, but we go to Bill's Fish Place tomorrow," I said.

Alicia nodded.

The fish and chips place turned out to be better than expected. Besides fish and chips, they offered crab and shrimp salads, clam chowder and the Tuesday Special—a slab of red snapper with cheese and bacon on a sesame seed bun. The rustic building consisted of a ring of windows surrounding a small kitchen and limited customer seating and facilities.

Alicia suggested we eat outside. We quickly found an empty table on the far side of the weathered deck that stretched directly over a large family of floating, snorting sea lions.

Kyle ordered cheese and bacon on a bun—hold the fish.

Alicia and I ordered fish and chips British style—hold the vinegar.

Waiting for handouts, multitudes of seagulls balanced on one foot, sometimes two, along the railing close to our table. I felt a little nervous as their beady eyes followed our every move from a mere six feet away.

When the three of us had finished our lunches, I paid the bill (an employee perk) and we left our seats to the birds. We stretched our legs a few paces and stopped suddenly at the sound of a ruckus behind us. Four seagulls beak-wrestled each other over crumbs as they danced on our plates. I wondered what birds did for food and entertainment before restaurants. Were they a kinder, gentler flock in those days?

We finally turned our backs on the food fight and walked back to the gallery where a multi-colored, hand-painted hippy van was being gutted by two young men, one black, one white, carrying a seven-foot tall bronze mermaid.

Out of curiosity, I followed the men into the windowless gallery. At first I was not aware that a beagle-boxer-terrier mix had followed me inside.

"Hey, get out of here!" Nico shouted from the back wall, fifty feet away."

I stiffened.

He clapped his hands and stomped his foot.

I froze. Then I turned and saw the dog behind me.

Nico took long steps, for a short man, shouting the whole way.

The collarless dog didn't move, just watched the little Greek guy pounding across the hardwood floor.

Nico stopped short of the dirty brown paws, waved his arms and yelled at the dog who was not easily ruffled.

"Get out, mutt—shoo, shoo."

The sad-eyed canine suddenly let out a bark worthy of a much bigger dog.

Nico jumped and stumbled backward, arms spinning into the guy behind him. Both guys lost control of the mermaid. They went down still holding onto the big fish. Irene leaped forward and grabbed the top end of the statue as it hit the floor.

Nico let out a groan.

"I'll take the dog outside…" I said, eager to leave the building.

Nico didn't answer. He was already ten feet away, studying the shiny hardwood floor for damage. He circled and muttered while Irene helped the men raise Ms. Mermaid to an upright position.

The mutt followed me out the door.

"Who's he?" Alicia asked from the third rung on her ladder.

"I don't know but he didn't make a very good impression on Nico." I grabbed a small bucket of paint, a three-inch brush and began the tedious job of painting between all eight columns of a not-crumbling Parthenon.

Kyle was close to halfway finished with his area along the top and Alicia had filled in almost as much in the midsection. The sun's heat penetrated the right side of my body, but being a competitive person with a strong work ethic I ignored the sun and painted at full speed until five o'clock. When Kyle made a comment about my red face, I finally realized that my skin felt stiff and prickly hot on one side.

As we folded and carried our ladders to the shed, Alicia gave me a long look and then a lecture on the consequences of not wearing sun block—easy for her to say with her naturally beautiful, tanned skin. I kept still because I knew Alicia had my best interests at heart.

"Jo, your face isn't just stiff, it's sad. What's going on?"

"I'm worried about Emmett going into depression again. He wasn't doing well this morning."

"Sorry to hear that. He's a nice man," she said, dropping a folded tarp over the ladder. "Sounds like you need to draw him out, you know, get him to tell you what's on his mind."

"Easier said than done, but you're right. I'll try harder. See you tomorrow." I climbed into my truck and sat for a minute, recharging my brain-battery. Between the hard work and hot sun, I was feeling my age and then some. I cruised through Moss Landing slowly, not feeling ready for Emmett's moods, but afraid to leave him alone for too long. I barely noticed the uneventful ride home.

My heart gave a happy thump as I rounded the one turn in my driveway and caught sight of David's Miata. I cut the engine and lumbered into the house.

Solow danced around my calves, whining a sweet hello.

"Josie...I, ah, just got here a minute ago. Can't seem to find Emmett. Isn't he supposed to...."

"...stay home...yes. He was sleeping when I left this morning, but he knows the rules."

"I'll drive us over to his property. The cops and fire inspector should be gone by now. You gotta give Emmett a little slack, honey—he's almost ninety." David put his arms around me and I instantly felt better. But as soon as we separated, the worries came right back.

I grabbed a leash, snapped it on Solow's collar and we climbed into the Miata. We could have walked, but riding was faster and David knew I was feeling anxious.

"Hold it, David, I want to collect the mail." I pulled four envelopes and three advertisements from Emmett's mail box and quickly read the return addresses before David had time to give me the ethical-eye.

"I want to know everything about Emmett so I can protect him," I said.

"Josie, it's not up to you to protect him. Leave that to the Sheriff's Department." He parked in the grass and we piled out.

Lilly bounded down the hill to greet us and check our pockets for treats. She gave me a friendly butt when I failed the treat test.

Solow gave one sharp bark. Lilly twirled around and galloped up the hill.

"Let's follow Lilly. Maybe she'll lead us to Hooley," I said.

"Look." David pointed to a metal box on top of the pile of charred sticks over grey ashes. "That must be the wall safe Deputy Sayer was talking about." The fortified box was the size of a microwave oven, partially melted and completely black. The well-cooked door gaped.

"If something was in the safe, it probably burned," David said.

"Or someone stole the contents and blew up the house." I'd seen enough. It was time to round up our friend. One problem, he was nowhere to be found. We checked the cottage and the grounds—nothing. We decided to go back to my house and check Emmett's room for clues.

The house was just as we left it—painfully quiet.

I charged up the stairs to Emmett's room. His bed was carefully made and his modest wardrobe hung in the closet. His letters were in a neat pile on the bureau. My heart raced. It seemed too good to be true. I rounded the bed and reached for the pile of letters.

Suddenly Solow howled, the front door opened and I heard David greeting Emmett.

I put the letters down, went to the rail and looked down. "Emmett, we've been looking for you." I forgot about his mail and thundered down the steps, anxious to hear his explanation.

"I called my dentist this morning to make an appointment," he grinned. "The dentist had an opening today so I called my friend, Rusty, and he drove me to the Watsonville office. He waited for me and when I was finished he drove me home."

I noticed immediately that the missing tooth had been replaced with a temp.

"This friend, Rusty, did you tell him where you live?" I asked.

"Of course, I told him. He had to pick me up," Emmett shrugged. "Rusty's my best friend."

"He's one more person...oh, never mind." I gave up trying to explain the danger, and walked to the kitchen in search of food for dinner. The boys sat down at the kitchen table and watched me chop vegetables. They offered to help. I refused the help. I needed my space. I chopped onions, carrots, bok choy, peppers and chicken for a fast stir fry. Every chop helped me eliminate stress.

David pushed away from the table, closed in behind me and gently took the knife from my hand.

"You're tired, Josie. I'll finish up here. You might want to put something on that sunburn."

I grabbed another knife and kept chopping as if it was a cure for exhaustion and frustration. But David was right. I was feeling the weight of Emmett's situation on my shoulders, not to mention a full day of painting in the hot sun. I finally let David chop while I took his place at the table.

Solow rested his head against my knee.

"Josephine, do you have aloe vera in your garden?" Emmett asked.

"Garden? What garden? Not the plant, if that's what you mean...."

"That's what I mean. After dinner, we can pick some aloe vera from my garden."

When dinner was over and the dishes were loaded into the dishwasher, David drove us down my driveway and started to turn left onto Otis. He suddenly hit the brakes as a white van shot down the road barely missing the jeep's front bumper.

"What's your hurry?" I snapped at the van, and Solow howled as it disappeared around a turn.

Moments later, we climbed out of the jeep on Hooley property.

Emmett led me to a row of aloe vera cactus growing beside the patio behind the house, that is, if the house hadn't burned down. He broke off a pointy, juicy section of cactus about eight inches long and handed it to me.

"Thank you, Emmett...oh, look what I found on the patio." I held up an old fashioned clip-on earring. A single pearl surrounded by little colorless sparkly stones shone in the light of the setting sun. "I guess this was your sister's?" My voice slipped down to a whisper.

Emmett pulled his eyebrows together as I dropped the lovely piece of jewelry into his hand.

"It was my mother's." He slipped the earring into his pocket.

"Shall we look around for the other earring?" I wondered if the path we stood on was the path Emmett walked on the night of the fire—the night someone ran into him in the dark.

Before he had time to answer, a little brown goat galloped up to us.

"Lilly! Come to Papa." Emmett hugged his little goat. "Maybe she'll follow us home," he laughed. Solow wiggled into the action, wagging his tail and half his body.

"Let's walk home," I said, "and see if Lilly follows us."

David said he wanted to drive home and make some phone calls. He kissed me on the cheek, ducked into his car and drove away.

Lilly galloped in frisky goat-circles all the way to my house.

I quickly furnished the shed with a bowl of water and an old blanket. I hoped the little nanny would stay and make Emmett happy. If she made my house her home, he would have one less reason to visit his property, making my job of keeping him safe a little easier.

CHAPTER EIGHT

I heard Emmett bumping around the house early Wednesday morning. We needed to talk. He'd fallen asleep on the couch right after dinner the night before. I'd gone to bed earlier than usual, hoping to wake up early and corner the old man over breakfast.

Showered and dressed, I moseyed down the hall to the kitchen where Mr. Hooley, Mr. Solow and Mr. Coffee greeted me.

"Good morning, young lady," Emmett said, handing me a mug of hot coffee. "We need to talk."

"Wow, you had me on, 'young lady.' I've been 'ma'amed' for so long I forgot what 'young lady' sounds like. I agree that we need to talk."

Emmett took a sip of jo and looked me in the eye. "Josephine, even though I pay you rent money, I feel like I'm imposing. I need to think about my future."

Wow, I thought, *he thinks about the future when he's eighty-nine years old?*

"If I stay here it will only be until I can arrange a home of my own. I deeply appreciate your hospitality, but I must rebuild my life." Emmett refilled my mug with a shaky hand. I ignored the puddles of java.

"Emmett, you're not imposing. I enjoy your company. I don't know what kind of house you want, but I think we need to talk about what happened to the last one—who blew up your house and why. I've been dying to ask you something."

Emmett cocked his head and raised an eyebrow.

"You seemed concerned about something in the stack of mail I handed you. Was there something that might point to the killer?"

He rubbed a finger across his dyed-black caterpillar mustache.

"No, no, nothing like that. But there was one piece of mail, a postcard that bothered me. Hilda's best friend and confidant, Rose Hymiller, lives in a convalescent home in Capitola. Her husband, my nephew, recently put her in the home because she was becoming forgetful. Hilda was very upset over that. I heard her on the telephone telling Ed, Rose's husband, that God wouldn't forgive what he'd done to Rose. Hilda scolded my nephew and told him that all he wanted was to sell the house so he could squander the money on his son who has no money-sense. The son is from Ed's first marriage."

"How old are Rose and Ed?"

"They're still young—only in their late sixties," he sighed, as if remembering when he was only sixty-something. "Rose is too young to be in a nursing home. She sent the postcard, bless her heart. She couldn't know that Hilda wouldn't be around to read it."

"So that's why you were upset?"

"The story is a little more complicated than that."

"What do you mean? Complicated?" I scratched my head.

"Over the years, Hilda periodically loaned money to Ed and Rose to help with their house payments. When Ed sold the house, Hilda was angry and told him to pay back the money. He refused. But she was never angry with Rose. In fact, she drove to the nursing home and demanded they release the poor woman. She thought Rose could stay with us, but rules are rules—yada yada, and they wouldn't let her leave without her husband's signature, and he wouldn't sign."

I tried to imagine eighty-seven-year-old Hilda taking care of sixty-something Rose.

"So, how old is the son?"

"Early forties with nothing to show for it—thinks he's a painter." Emmett rolled his eyes to the ceiling.

"Emmett, more coffee?"

"No thank you, Josephine. I'm going to work on clocks today. I need a steady hand."

"That's great, Emmett. I'm glad you have a project. I thought you said you didn't have any family around here."

"You asked about Hooleys. Rose and Ed are Hymillers. Ed's father, my cousin, immigrated to the USA shortly after the war with me as his sponsor and employer. As a family, we're not close. My cousin died many years ago and his son, my nephew, Ed, is irresponsible. We helped them financially over the years. It was our duty. Now I feel no responsibility. Hilda wouldn't want me to help Ed in any way."

"Is there anyone else you haven't mentioned?"

"Josephine, I didn't mention Ed at first because he's not worth mentioning." Emmett stood as if to leave the room.

"Emmet, sit down…please. I want to help you find the murderer, but I need to know about all the possible suspects, especially people you don't like or that don't like you. We need to work together on this."

"I understand, Josephine. If I think of anyone, I'll tell you." He walked out the back door and sat on a bench facing the sunrise.

I prepared a decent breakfast and Emmett ate his share. I wanted to fatten him up and evaluate his mood, always afraid he'd fall into another funk. Even

I teetered on a bad mood now and then as the murder business kept us dancing around a dangerous situation we didn't understand.

"Emmett, why don't you make a list of possible suspects? Just jot down names of people you think might have wanted to hurt you or Hilda. We can go over the list when I get home from work."

He nodded, absentmindedly shoving his last bite of waffle through a puddle of syrup.

"I can't read your mind, Hooley, so you really need to do this, OK?"

"OK," he mumbled as I gathered my phone, purse, sunscreen and large brimmed straw hat, and headed out the door.

The truck cab was toasty warm, a wonderful thing after so many foggy mornings. I cruised through Aromas and then sped west on San Juan Road. As I drove toward Moss Landing, I tried to remember every detail concerning Rose's husband, Ed, and placed him on my "Potential Murderer List," right under Gertrude and Arnie. I swung a right into the tiny harbor town of Moss Landing, pulled in next to Alicia's Volvo and cut the engine.

She walked up to my window. "Good morning, Jo. Kyle just called." She snapped her phone shut. "He's going to a doctor appointment at ten and won't be here until noon."

"Infected piercing, itchy tattoo, chaffing ankle bracelet?"

"Trouble with the nose-ring."

"Figures! Looks like we're the only ones here," I said, looking across the parking lot. "Well, let's get set up and start painting the shadows."

Alicia led the way to the shed. We hauled every ladder and piece of equipment to the front sidewalk and spread tarps over the rosemary bushes. We mixed up three shades of muted purple, the darkest being almost black, and filled our palettes.

"Allie, I'll lay in the lighter shadows. You follow me and darken the deeper recesses." We knew the drill. The basic principles were always the same but every mural and every subject had its individual idiosyncrasies and surprising outcome.

By noon, we'd shaded large areas.

When we finished the shading, I fished around in my purse for my little hand mirror, crossed the street, turned my back to the mural and raised the mirror until I was able to see the painting behind me. The new shadows seemed to push the unpainted pillars forward. The illusion was already working.

Kyle arrived on his motorcycle wearing a bandage under his freckled nose. His sunburn looked worse than mine, or was he blushing because of his bandage? He shed his leather chaps and hung his helmet on a handlebar.

I recrossed the narrow street. "Hey Kyle, you're just in time to go to lunch."

"Like, I'm on antibiotics," he groaned, looking pitiful as a stray puppy.

Alicia laughed and pulled Kyle by his arm. "Come on, Kyle, we're going to Bill's."

We eagerly marched past half a dozen businesses to the fish restaurant. Kyle brought up the rear. I knew he wasn't wild about fish but he always appreciated a free lunch. Bill's menu was ninety-nine percent fish and one percent grilled-cheese sandwiches. Alicia and I were thrilled with the choices. Kyle seemed happy with a double order of grilled-cheese sandwiches, pickles on the side.

Bill's had its own assemblage of feisty seagulls sharing space with the public on the wrap-around-deck. Lapping water, snorting sea lions, chugging trawlers and squabbling gulls kept our conversation to a minimum, but the salmon salad was exquisite.

"Allie, what do you think of the paintings Kat delivered today?"

"I watched a documentary where elephants did similar work but with prettier colors," she said. "Actually, I like the paintings more than the delivery woman. I know it was an accident, but she could have apologized. If I kicked over a bucket of paint I'd stop everything and help clean it up…and then she made purple footprints across Dino's beautiful floor. I thought he'd explode. Good thing we were there to wipe the floor before the paint dried."

"I guess that modern art stuff sells," I said, "or it wouldn't make it into a nice gallery like this one. I like the mermaid statue, but where do you put a thing like that? For sixty-five thousand dollars, guess I won't be buying it any time soon."

"Jo, guess what. I took your suggestion and asked Trigger if he'd like to look up the names of some people for me. If he's successful, I'll tell him who the people are. If he doesn't find them it won't matter anyway. But you're right, he does enjoy the challenge."

"That's wonderful, Alicia. I hope he finds them." I paid the lunch bill and we walked back to the gallery where another delivery was in progress. This delivery had me drooling over five large watercolor paintings.

At the end of the day, I went inside to check them out.

"Josephine, how do you like Roy's….?" Irene began. I turned away from the modern canvases leaning against the wall, to the watercolors waiting to be hung.

"These paintings are so beautiful," I swooned, not wanting to give an opinion on the over-sized elephant-works. But my long-ago art teachers would have loved them. The paintings were everything they espoused—loose, loose and looser. I admired a loose style if the painting pulled me in, made a statement or touched my heart. But Kat had delivered dark distressing canvases I'd rather forget.

Alicia walked up behind me. "Lovely watercolor paintings, don't you think?"

"Yes, I love them. I met Bonni Carver once, very talented lady."

"What do you think of those?" Allie thumbed Roy's mostly black, red and blue slaps of paint.

"Allie, you know me pretty well...."

"Yes I do, and I feel the same." She turned away from Irene and wrinkled her nose at me. We'd let the real art-critics judge, namely the general public who vote with their money.

Irene walked us out the door and locked up the building.

Nico was already in the Mercedes talking on the phone.

As Kyle roared out of town, I said goodbye to Alicia and climbed into my truck. My body was one big ache from elbows to knees. I wondered if I was getting too old to be painting for long periods of time. When I was a young girl, I fantasized about being a private detective, thanks to the Nancy Drew series. But having no formal training in that area, I'd have to stick to my love of painting.

I sat in the Mazda, rolled down the window and motored through Moss Landing, welcoming the soft touch of moist air against my face. Evening fog had already gobbled up the sun and would engulf the harbor in mere minutes. The fishing boats had been hosed down and parked in their berths hours ago. They rocked with the rhythm of the water, slow and gentle, side to side, waiting for the all-encompassing mist to tuck them in for the night.

Even though I was exhausted from a long day of painting, I felt good about our progress on the mural. It was amazing how the pillars pushed forward so early in the process. The techniques we used were tried and true, but the results always took me by surprise.

We were getting to know our employers and they were turning out to be very interesting people. Irene was the talkative one—a bit of a motor-mouth, actually. She was ten years old when their family immigrated to America from Greece and Nico was twelve. After grade school and college, they managed a Sausalito Gallery until they were finally able to invest in their own business. Their parents coughed up some money, giving them a half interest in the project. Irene was easy-going while Nico had his undies in a permanent twist. But he seemed to like the mural, so I was happy.

I made the usual left turn up my driveway, put my thoughts aside and became aware of the fact that smoke was coming out of the chimney. I only used the little cast iron wood stove in the winter to keep the gas bill down. Why would anyone burn in the summer? I opened the front door and walked into the toasty front room.

Solow galloped through the house to greet me.

"Miss Josephine, hope you don't mind the fire," Emmett said, looking comfy in the rocking chair.

"Not at all, Mr. Hooley. I'll just open a window for a little fresh air." As I opened a window in the kitchen I thought I saw someone or something moving through the wild lilac bushes along Otis near the front corner of my property. My heart did a fast rumba until I told myself it was probably a family of deer making their way up the road to Emmett's apple trees. But the initial thing that had caught my eye was a one second glint, like the sun hitting metal. I put the thought aside, poured two glasses of iced tea and carried them to the living room.

"Thank you," Emmett said, as I handed him a glass. "I was feeling cold after my nap, but I'm all right now. I'm letting the fire go out."

"The fog is headed this way," I said. "In an hour or so, we'll be glad for the warmth. Emmett, have you seen deer or other animals around the property today...or anything unusual?"

"No. I've been busy working on clocks and such. I don't think I've been outside today."

"Do you have a list for me?"

He cocked his head.

"You know—a list of people who might want to hurt you and Hilda."

"Oh, that, yes. I did jot down a few names. But I don't think any of these people would actually hurt me."

"Well, we have to start somewhere," I said.

Hooley climbed the stairs to his room. When he came back, he handed me a pink post-it with three names clearly printed on it. The first was, Fahima.

I asked who Fahima was.

"She's married to my friend, Rusty. I called Rusty today. He offered to let me stay at his house in Watsonville. I didn't give him a definite answer...his wife would be difficult to live with."

"Why do you say that?"

"She hates the fact that I'm Jewish."

"What's her problem?"

"Fahima is from the Middle East," he shrugged. "I think it's cultural."

"You definitely don't want to live there, Hooley. Besides, I like having you here. But I don't understand why Fahima's on your list? Did she do something ...?"

"...bad? Not really, but she always thought Hilda hated her. I think Fahima felt rejected by my sister, but Hilda had her own friends. Fahima has no friends—even her children and grandchildren stay away from her."

"How did you meet Rusty?"

"Rusty and I go way back to the forties when I went into the clock business. His father owned a small hardware store on Monterey Avenue in San Jose. He was behind on the mortgage so he rented a corner of his store to me. I had just enough room to repair clocks. Eventually I moved into a larger store, but good old Rusty and his father gave me a start when no one else would."

"Sounds like your rent money helped to keep him in business."

"Yes, I guess you could say that. I only stayed one year because Fahima didn't like me."

"Oh, why?"

"Who knows such things? I only know Fahima is not a pleasant person."

"OK...we'll keep her on the list. How about number two, your cousin, Ed Hymiller?"

"There's a feud that goes back to the nineteen thirties in Germany when my grandfather chose between two sons. He chose to give my father the secret recipe for beer. My father's brother was outraged and that feeling was passed down to his oldest son, Ed, who's tried to extract the recipe from me for years. The harder he tries, the more I refuse."

I looked into Emmet's face. "The recipe is in the box you wanted to bury...right?"

"It's written on the box, carved into the lid. Many years ago, Ed tried to make a deal with me. He wanted to sell the recipe to a big brewery for lots of money. The more he pushed, the tighter I held onto my inheritance. We've never been friends."

"OK. Now, number three. Why, Arnie?"

"Because he knows Gertrude. She's Ed's ex-wife and the mother of Ed's son. I get along with her and we talk together sometimes. You know how women talk...ah, but not you, of course. I don't know why, but every time Gertrude asks a question, I end up telling her all kinds of things."

"Does she know about the recipe?"

"Yes, and the jewels." Emmett looked at the floor as if he'd misbehaved.

"What jewels?"

"They were my mother's. She came from a wealthy family. The family business involved a diamond mine in Africa." His words hung in the air like an atomic explosion.

"Are the jewels in the wooden box?"

"Yes, except for the ones Hilda kept in her jewelry box upstairs. The earring you found came from her room. Whoever ran into me in the dark must have dropped it."

"What about the empty safe I saw in the rubble?"

"We never used it," he sighed. "I used a hidden compartment in the wooden box instead. I kept the box in the cottage. If someone found it they would think it was just a place to keep the carving tools."

I nodded, remembering the first time I saw the box.

"Why didn't you tell the police about your jewels?"

"I'm not in a hurry. I'd rather wait until I know who did it."

"Actually, I'm not very good at giving up facts either," I laughed. "Just ask the deputies. But I am in a hurry. We have to find out who's after you and why."

CHAPTER NINE

Thursday morning happened in the blink-of-an-eye. I lay in bed remembering a perfect evening the night before. Emmett had fallen asleep on the sofa. I had ducked out the back door with Solow and a flashlight. The waning moon poked through patches of fog and a barn owl startled me with a well-timed hoot. I had tramped through the grassy field between my house and David's, confident Solow would protect me from unfriendly animals.

Yellow light flooded David's patio when he heard Solow's happy howls. He cracked open the sliding glass door and invited us in. We talked for awhile, discussing Emmett's family and friends. I told David about Rusty, Fahima, Gertrude, Arnie and poor old Rose. We put our heads together trying to guess at issues and motives.

David didn't think anything we discussed would be a motive for murder. I didn't think so either.

We had a glass of wine, cuddled closer and talked about the mural project. When all the talking was done, we simply enjoyed each other's company, and when the clock struck twelve we kissed goodbye in the doorway.

Solow led me home under a smiling moon.

I finally put pleasant remembrances aside, pulled myself out of bed and dressed for another strenuous day of painting.

Emmett sat at the kitchen table, unusually quiet as he ran his thumb up and down his coffee mug. He checked the clock on the wall every couple minutes and barely touched the breakfast I prepared. He asked if he could carry anything to the truck for me.

"Thanks, Hooley, but it's just me and my purse today. Is everything OK?"

"Certainly."

"See you around five," I said, ruffling Solow's fur. If I'd tarried, I think the old gentleman would have hauled me out to the truck all by himself. Maybe he was anxious to be alone to work on clocks.

As soon as I reached Moss Landing, I called Emmett to make sure he was all right. The line was busy. The next time I called was on our lunch break. No one answered.

"Jo, what's the matter?" Alicia asked.

"Nothing, I hope. Finish your grilled-cheese sandwich, Kyle, so we can get back to work."

"Ouch! What's eating you, Jo?" Alicia cocked her head to one side while Kyle masticated the second half of his second sandwich.

I paid the bill.

Kyle ran a napkin across his goatee a couple times as he followed us down the sidewalk to the Parthenon where a delivery was in progress. This time it was furniture—an over-sized black lacquer and glass case as long as my truck and twice as tall. It arrived in four pieces, but was fully assembled by the time we were ready to go home. Nico walked us outside.

"We're negotiating with Chihuly…."

"The real...Chihuly?" I stammered.

"Yes, we hope to show several of his pieces…."

"Allie, can you believe it? I can't wait to see his work right here in this gallery!" Suddenly I worried about the Parthenon—was it good enough? I'd seen a

Chihuly show in San Francisco. His work was indescribable—except to say the pieces were large, colorful, fanciful, hand-blown glass creations that had me drooling.

I was so excited about Chihuly's art coming to the Halikias Gallery, I completely forgot to worry about Emmett. I was almost home before I remembered that he hadn't answered the phone.

I opened my front door. Solow galloped across the room and circled my legs a dozen times while I called Emmett's name. No answer. I heard gravel crunching, twirled around and stepped outside.

A thirty-year-old pock-marked maroon Oldsmobile lumbered to a stop behind my truck, barely tapping the bumper. The engine coughed twice and went silent. Two grey heads were visible through the dusty windshield. I took a few steps toward the car and saw Hooley in the back seat. Three doors opened at once and the old folks slowly emerged. The driver stretched as if he'd been driving for hours.

"You must be Josephine. Emmett told us you were a pretty young lady," the old blue-eyed gentleman grinned. His toupee needed adjusting, but his smile was charming.

"Yes, I'm Josephine…and you are…?

"Rusty."

A thin, hunched old woman climbed out of the passenger seat and circled behind the car like a drunk in an earthquake, over to Rusty's side.

"And this is my wife, Fahima. Steady old girl," he warned, grabbing her elbow.

Solow sniffed the woman's ankle-length skirt.

She grazed him with her foot.

Emmett joined the group.

In one quick movement, my devoted basset whipped his long body around, accidentally whacking the woman's legs with his tail as he tried to greet Emmett.

Fahima teetered and fell to the ground, landing on her undercarriage. Emmett and Rusty each took an arm and hauled her into a standing position.

"Are you all right, Fahima?" I asked.

She grunted, turned around and shuffled back to the passenger seat.

Rusty explained to me that his wife was prone to falling. He asked if I'd like to ride up to Emmett's property in the Oldsmobile. Hooley wanted to collect his mail and Rusty was curious about the ash pile.

I tried to cover my fear of riding in a car with three seniors whose ages added up to almost three-hundred.

"Actually, I have a couple things I want to do first—I'll meet you up there."

Emmett opened the back seat door. Solow climbed in and Emmett followed.

Rusty cranked up the eight-cylinder engine after three noisy turns of the key.

I walked into the house, not wishing to witness Rusty's backing up skills. Feeling tired, hungry and a bit cranky, I had no desire to go anywhere. But I'd promised so I trudged up Otis, hoping to be back home shortly.

As I rounded the third turn in the road a white van shot out of Hooley's driveway and barely missed me as I leaped into the brush. My heart was pounding. The smell of burnt rubber permeated the air. I stood up and brushed off my backside.

"What was that about?" I said to myself as I walked up Hooley's driveway on wobbly legs.

The Oldsmobile, with three doors gaping, sat quietly a few yards from the remains of Hooley's home. The old folks climbed out of their seats and gazed in the direction of the mail box.

I walked up to Emmett and asked what happened.

"Nothing, really. A white van was parked down there by the mailbox. We didn't see anyone in it so we drove up here and parked. All of a sudden, the engine started, the van circled and went that way. The windows were tinted so we couldn't see who was driving."

I put a hand on Hooley's shoulder. "I think we should find the van and get a license number. Rusty, can I borrow your car?"

"Certainly. Come on everyone, climb in!" Rusty said, and handed over the keys. We scrambled into our seats. The last thing I wanted was to worry about passengers, but it was too late to protest.

Solow shared the back seat with Rusty and Emmett.

Fahima sat in the front, fussing over her seat belt. For the sake of speed, I snapped it for her, but she fussed again when I hit a speed bump at thirty miles an hour and again when we ran a stop sign at the end of Otis. The mighty Olds roared and Fahima shrieked as I stomped on the accelerator, drowning out the elevator music on the radio. The boys in the back made encouraging noises and Solow howled long and hard.

There was no sign of a white van, which left us three choices; go straight to Gilroy, turn left to Watsonville or turn around and go home. There wasn't time to gather a consensus. I made a hard left at the intersection causing Fahima to slam against the door. She pulled herself up straight, then screamed and pointed at the back end of a white van as it disappeared around a turn two blocks ahead.

Rusty leaned forward and shouted in my ear. "Get him, Josephine! Hurry!"

"Hold on, back there...speed bumps...whoa ...everyone OK?"

"Go, Josephine," Emmett shouted. "We're all right."

Solow barked as he stretched his long body over Emmett's lap and pressed his nose against the window.

I glanced in the rearview mirror. The guys were bouncing around like whirligigs and Rusty's rug was missing. We flew over two more speed bumps and careened onto Aromas Road for a quick quarter of a mile. I turned right onto San Juan Road and stomped on the gas peddle, bringing the needle up to seventy for the straight stretch. We bounced and jerked over three sets of railroad tracks and passed two cars.

Fahima had a white-knuckle grip on the door as she leaned toward the dash. Through thick lenses, her eyes searched the road ahead. But after a couple of really fast miles, I realized we'd lost the van. It must have turned left when we turned right onto San Juan.

Fahima looked as disappointed as I felt.

The boys were quiet—even Solow shifted his position and settled down for a nap.

Feeling disappointed that we didn't get a license plate number, I cut our speed down to a legal fifty-five and cruised down the straight two-lane road between fields of lettuce and strawberries.

"Are you folks hungry?" I asked.

"I am very hungry," Fahima said, wearing a broad grin which made me wonder if she'd enjoy the Giant Dipper Rollercoaster at the boardwalk or maybe skydiving lessons.

"I'm hungry too," Rusty said, rearranging his toupee. "Let's all go to the Smorgy on Beach Street."

"Yes indeed, if Josephine doesn't mind driving," Emmett said.

"I don't mind at all. I think I'm getting the hang of this big old car." Solow snored as I calmly drove toward the setting sun. I heard more snorts from the front seat, and glanced at Fahima with her head back, eyes closed and mouth open. By the time we reached Smorgy's in Santa Cruz, I was the only one awake. Not wishing to navigate "the big boat" into a parking space for compact cars, I chose an empty space at the far end of the lot.

Fahima opened her eyes and raised her head. "Where are we?"

"Smorgy's, time to wake up back there," I announced. "Don't worry about Solow. He'll be happy to stay here and have another nap."

The guys opened their doors and climbed out. Everyone seemed happy to be standing on terra firma, myself included. My gaggle of geezers shuffled into the restaurant.

Rusty and Emmett stood at the front desk and split the tab (pay first—eat later).

A young woman led us to an empty table.

"Josephine, we start over here," Rusty said, pointing to acres of carbohydrates.

Fahima took my arm and led the way. We lined up at the first food station where each person took a wet plate and a handful of silverware. We moved along the counter to a large roast tanning under a heat lamp. An unshaven man wearing a tall white chef's hat carved off a thin slice of beef and dropped it on my plate.

"Two slices, please," Rusty said. The chef dropped two pink slabs on Rusty's plate. "And two for my friend." He pointed to Emmett and two pieces of meat were dropped on his plate. Moving along, we helped ourselves to enchiladas, baked potatoes, slices of pizza, pasta salad, and a dozen more calorie-loaded delights. Our plates were not large so the food piled higher and higher.

Fahima peered over her fully loaded plate as she led us toward our table. Suddenly an elderly gentleman pushed his chair back from his table. Her plate hit squarely on the man's bald head. Fahima teetered and started to fall back.

"I got ya," I said as I caught her arm while balancing my plate with the other hand.

The man wiped his head with a napkin, stood up and marched to the men's room without a word.

Rusty quickly rounded Fahima and held her other arm until we had her settled in a chair.

Emmett looked overwhelmed as he placed his loaded plate on the table and sat down.

"Fahima, don't worry, I'll fix a plate for you." I put my plate down on the table, crossed the room and began to gather food. The chef frowned when I held out the new plate, but a pink slab was delivered. I was already familiar with the various offerings and darted from station to station collecting a variety of foods.

Fahima smiled when I set the plate in front of her.

"Thank you, Josephine, but where is the bread?"

"I'll find it," I said. After searching through four different food stations I finally gave up and told her it was all gone.

She groaned and went back to her tamale pie.

My stomach growled. At that point I was hungry enough to lick the food off the bald man's head. My food was barely warm, but I ate until I thought I would pop a button.

The guys quickly cleaned their plates. They sat back in their chairs looking like glassy-eyed toads, barely able to stay awake while Fahima worked on her cream of halibut and cold French fries.

"Can I get you anything else, Fahima?" I asked.

She shook her head and kept chewing.

"Fahima, how do you like living in San Jose?" I asked.

She took a moment to swallow. "We moved to Watsonville over twenty years ago."

"Do you like living there?"

Fahima shrugged her narrow shoulders.

I finally gave up trying to make conversation. It was eight-thirty and I was exhausted. We left the building and began our slow trek across the parking lot, bathed in artificial yellow light. Halfway home Rusty mentioned the fact that he was unable to drive at night.

"Can Fahima drive at night?"

"Fahima doesn't drive."

Emmett cleared his throat. "Rusty, why don't you and the Missus sleep in my cottage tonight and drive home in the morning? The place has two cots, running water and a toilet.

Rusty looked at Fahima who had acquired a droopy-eyed stare. Since she didn't object, Rusty said they'd be glad to stay in Emmett's cottage for the night.

I drove the Olds to Emmett's house and waited in the car while he led Rusty and his wife to the hidden cabin.

I settled back and listened to oldies music on the radio as the sky darkened, stars became visible and a slice of moon rose up from the east.

Emmett's flashlight waggled down the path toward the car. Solow whined with excitement as the old man climbed into the back seat with my dog.

"Hooley, what happens in the morning? Do they want me to bring the car back here?"

"That would be nice, Josephine."

I fired up all eight cylinders, sending an explosion of bad air out the tail pipe. Two minutes later we were parked in front of my house beside David's Jeep.

Emmett opened his door and Solow leaped to the ground, sniffing his way around the Jeep.

"Come on, old buddy, let's go inside." I opened the front door, and Solow charged past me.

Emmett trundled up the drive and entered the house.

David welcomed me with a warm hug. He asked if we would like some freshly popped popcorn.

"Thanks, David, but I won't be eating anything for at least a month." I groaned and rubbed my stomach for effect.

Emmett laughed and said he felt the same way.

"Did you see how much Fahima ate? I think I put too much on her plate and she thought she should eat all of it."

"I have never seen her eat like that," Emmett said. "And I have never seen her being courteous to anyone until tonight. I think she wants to be your friend, Josephine."

"She's not the most likable person, but she sure likes my driving. Too bad you weren't there, David."

"I wasn't invited."

"Oh, it was a last minute decision," I explained. "You see, I walked up the road to Hooley's place and this white van came shooting down the road and almost ran over me. It was coming from Emmett's property. We decided to follow it and get a license plate number."

"Why does that not surprise me?"

"Well, we must have made a wrong turn because the van disappeared—so we went to Smorgy's for dinner."

"You wanted a license number because...?"

"Because the van was parked on Hooley's property—right next to the mailbox."

"Anything missing?" David asked.

"We forgot to look."

CHAPTER TEN

Friday started off with a bang—the bang of the front door, several rounds of "good morning" type greetings, old folks shuffling toward the kitchen and a basset tail pounding the floor.

By the time I showered and dressed, David had the morning meal ready. I was the last to take a seat at the table, just in time to hear Rusty and Emmett talking about a trip they were planning. They had their plane tickets to Arizona and planned to attend the Grand Fiftieth Cuckoo Clock Convention. They were revved up and ready to celebrate fifty years of cuckoo construction and innovation in America. The men sat on the edge of their seats, fantasizing about their trip while Fahima growled in another language.

"Fahima, what will you do while the boys are gone?" I asked, trying to lift her spirits.

"Practice the throwing of the darts," she said, with no attempt to rein in her Arab accent.

"Oh." The hair on the back of my head prickled. I put our dirty plates in the sink for a rinse, said my goodbyes, grabbed my purse and drove to Moss Landing in light traffic.

I parked next to the Halikias' Mercedes and helped Alicia drag our paint supplies out to the sidewalk.

Kyle arrived in time to help lay the tarps and set up the ladders.

From there, it was paint your brains out all day and head home exhausted.

The drive home gave me time to think about all we'd accomplished so far and all that still needed to be done. I described the unfinished Parthenon to Emmett when I got home. He said he'd like to see it someday. I offered to drive him over there the next day but he shook his head and said he'd be in Arizona.

"You mean you're really going to Arizona with Rusty?"

"No, he'll drive me to the airport but I'm going alone. Fahima said she'd kill her husband if he went to a girly convention."

"Is it a girly convention?"

"No."

"Hooley, you can't go by yourself. Someone wants to kill you. What if…?"

"…someone tries to kill me?" he said. "At least I don't have to live with a wife who wants to kill me," he laughed.

"Yes, but I can't let you go alone all the way to…."

"…Arizona." He looked at me and smiled. "Josephine, I have a wonderful idea. Hilda was going to go to the convention with me like we do every year. I offered her ticket to Rusty. You can use Hilda's ticket. We'll be back Tuesday night." His eyes twinkled as he smoothed his mustache.

How could I say "no?"

Hooley pulled two plane tickets out of his pocket and danced around the kitchen like the Irishman he was named after. A pipe and a pint were all that was missing.

I played with the idea of missing work Monday and Tuesday. Maybe my painters would like a long weekend and maybe the Halikiases wouldn't mind since the project was off to a good start. But the practical entrepreneur in me didn't like the idea of missing work.

To go or not to go, that was the question. I argued with myself, trying to see all sides. Just because I traveled with Emmett didn't mean I would for sure be able to keep him out of harm's way. But if I stayed home, there would be no way to help him.

"OK, Hooley, but just this once."

Emmett smiled as his new athletic shoes padded around the table for the third time. He dropped into a chair next to me breathing hard, promising to show me all around Black Canyon City, Arizona.

I asked where Black Canyon City was located. He told me it was in the middle of the state. I wanted to go to the Grand Canyon, but he thought it would be too far. I wanted to see Sedona but he said we wouldn't have time. I wanted to shop in Phoenix but he said the convention would be more interesting.

I rolled my eyes, imagining a room full of cuckoo clock makers comparing various springs and whistles, pumped up with Kool Aid and accordion music.

Emmett handed me Hilda's ticket.

"Hooley, this ticket says we leave at 7:00 o'clock in the morning."

"That's right. Is that inconvenient for you, Josephine?"

"I guess not. We'll have to get up at four o'clock in the morning and leave Aromas by four-thirty so we can be at the airport an hour and a half before take-off...which means we have to go to bed right away. But I have to pack and call Alicia and Kyle...and David...and Mom...and the Halikiases.... And you have to tell Rusty not to pick us up. I'll drive." My head swam with "things to do." What should I pack? Arizona in May would be an oven. What does one wear to a cuckoo convention anyway? I tried to remember if my truck had enough gas.

Emmett called Southwest Airlines, had Rusty's ticket transferred into my name and printed the new ticket using my computer and printer before I finished my first phone call. David didn't say much at first, but I could feel the tension through the receiver. He asked a few questions and advised me to stay home. But that was David, my gallant protector. He meant well. In the end he promised to take good care of Solow and Lilly.

Four more calls and a quick dinner of canned soup and I was ready to pack. I stuffed four outfits, pajamas, underwear, cosmetics, hand lotion and a can of pepper spray into my medium-size black suitcase with wheels. I gave the smaller matching case to Emmett knowing he didn't own many clothes. My bag had a sunflower sticker stuck to the bottom end and Emmett's wore an American flag sticker.

Solow watched me with knowing eyes as I set the alarm clock and climbed into bed. He usually pouted when my routine changed. This was a big pout occasion. I knew he knew that I was going away. I felt his sad-eyed night-vision staring from across the dark bedroom. My mind bounced from Solow to Lilly to Emmett's property. Would the van be back? Was Emmett's mail the target? Too many questions and too little time for sleep.

The pressure to hurry up and sleep had me wide awake. I glanced at the clock. Nine minutes had passed. Deciding that a glass of water would help me to sleep, I padded down the hall into the kitchen. A sliver of moonlight helped me to navigate the kitchen without turning on a light.

Something moved near the back door.

I froze. All I could hear was the pounding of my heart.

"Josephine, did you get up to see the moon?" Emmett asked.

"No, I just wanted a glass of water. What about you?"

"Couldn't sleep so I decided to nibble on leftover chicken."

I switched on a light.

Emmett blinked, took a last bite from the drumstick and tossed the bone in the garbage.

I pulled out a tub of rocky road ice cream and two spoons. We talked about the convention. Mostly, I asked questions and Emmett answered. He described each day's agenda, named off the people he knew and told me the ones to avoid.

He yawned.

I yawned.

We trundled off to bed.

My clock radio interrupted a splendid dream. David had asked me to dance at the Mushroom Festival. We twirled around giant fungi as the Tijuana Brass Band played "Waltzing Matilda." I finally pulled out of the dream and slapped the radio off. I conjured up the last dance, smiled and rolled out of bed. I checked the clock twice to make sure it was four o'clock. It felt more like midnight.

Solow kicked his legs, probably dreaming about a good cat chase.

I dressed in front of a small nightlight, not wishing to wake my sweet basset.

I bumped into Emmett in the hallway.

Gentleman Emmett insisted I use the bathroom first so I did. From there I moved into the kitchen and rustled up a light breakfast.

We ate, rolled our suitcases to the truck and left town before Solow knew we were gone.

The coastal fog thinned and disappeared. There was no sign of a sunrise as we motored northeast on Highway 101—just headlights, taillights and twinkly stars.

An hour later, we arrived at the San Jose Mineta International Airport. I dropped Emmett at the Southwest Airlines entrance and circled the airport back to the economy parking lot ten blocks from civilization. Half of Silicon Valley's workforce arrived at that same moment making parking difficult. I pulled into a tight space, locked the truck and hopped a shuttle bus back to Southwest.

Business folks working in San Jose routinely visited their field offices in LA, San Diego, Phoenix and fifty other cities. They basically traveled for a living, wearing suits and headphones, carrying a briefcase with one hand and pulling a suitcase with the other. They rarely talked to each other because they were usually texting or phoning bosses and clients. The regular public, like me, stood out in our colorful carefree clothing and panicked looks.

I was ready to panic until I spotted Emmett sitting on a bench just inside the entrance doors.

He stood up and we moved across the room to the beginning of the cattle corral where we inched along a path of zigzagging ropes attached to four-foot poles. I counted the people ahead of us and multiplied that by three minutes. At that rate we would be at the counter by Sunday. But Southwest proved me wrong and we checked our bags with time to spare.

Thanks to moving walkways and escalators we arrived at the second cattle containment in time to watch a rickety old woman in a wheel chair stand up in front of an x-ray machine, arms waving, body tipping side to side. Her ATF coach patiently waited for her to practice the pose until it was acceptable for a picture.

"Hooley, let's get out of here," I said, pulling at his sleeve. We stepped out of the line, veering off to the right into another line where a grumpy looking man was being wanded. We took our chances with wanding. It seemed better than giant x-rays or groping hands. The man with the wand ignored us and went for the redhead with the great tan behind me.

I put my flip flops and purse in a plastic bin and watched it being sucked into the x-ray machine. I steadied Emmett as he pulled off his new shoes and put them in a bin. A couple minutes later I helped him back into his shoes and tied the laces.

"Thank you, Josephine. Hilda always did that for me. I don't bend easily like you ladies."

"Glad to help. Now, which way?"

"Gate 23, that way." He shuffled out to the main hall that was about fifty feet wide and at least a mile long. We arrived at Gate 23 in time to fall in behind the last five boarders. The plane had one aisle with three rows of seats on each side. Out of 137 seats, 135 were already full. Emmett pointed out an empty seat for me and then he found one for himself four rows down the aisle. I watched him skinny into a seat between giggling fat lady twins with bouncy hair.

My seat was between a middle-aged man in the aisle seat and a familiar looking woman wearing her graying hair in a bun.

The man moved his legs to one side.

I stepped over the legs, settled into my middle seat and turned to the woman at the window.

"Gertrude, what are you...? I mean, aren't you Gertrude from the bank?" I asked, as my face suddenly overheated. I dabbed my forehead with a tissue.

"I work in a bank. How did you know?"

"I saw you there when I took my friend, Mr. Hooley, to your bank. Do you remember me? My name is Josephine Stuart."

"You look familiar. Nice to meet you, Josephine." She turned her head back to the window to watch the take-off. From there she fell asleep reading a magazine.

We arrived in Phoenix less than two hours later. By the time we collected our luggage, caught a shuttle to the car rental area and rented a bright yellow Jeep (Emmett's dream car), it was ten-thirty. We bought water, fruit and peanuts at a concession stand.

Emmett looked more alive and bright-eyed than I felt. Even his walking pace had been faster than usual but slower than anyone else' at the airport. But he was older than anyone else. He had an excuse. He gave me driving instructions as we munched on peanuts.

We sailed north on Highway 17 like a seventy-mile-an-hour tumbleweed in a wind storm. We passed oceans of desert and a few roadside towns. Emmett warned me to slow down and take the 434 exit. We veered off the highway on the exit ramp that ended with a cattle rattle, a metal grate to keep cows and donkeys from entering the highway. We had a choice of left or right.

Emmett pointed left.

I cranked the wheel to the left, crossed over the freeway and made a right onto a two-lane road heading north. We passed by an old motel, a gas station, an Amish restaurant, a Mom-and-Pop grocery store and several modest neighborhoods clustered around schools and churches.

"OK, Hooley, where's Black Canyon City?"

"That was it. It's a lot like Aromas, except for the convention center on the top of that hill over there." He pointed north.

"You're sure about that?" I stared across the vacant simmering landscape of hills, washes and cacti. Some of the hills were big enough to be small mountains, but by California standards they were still just hills.

A mile later, we were circling around another cactus-speckled hillside when something caught my eye. I looked across a wide wash to an odd structure ensconced in the side of a flat-top mountain about half a mile away. The structure matched the ochre of the earth around it. It was the large American flag that originally caught my attention. I watched a delivery truck climb the winding road leading to the opening in the hillside.

Our Jeep rolled across a section of straight highway and then we began to climb to the top of the flat-top mountain. A silver luxury SUV and a white stretch-limo followed us up the curvy road to a five-acre square of concrete on top. The parking lot was half full. Metal-framed glass shelters the size of one-car garages marked the four corners of the lot.

Emmett motioned for me to park near one of the tinted glass structures.

I pulled into a marked space and the SUV squeezed in beside us. A couple more cars arrived as we climbed out of the Jeep for a good stretch.

Emmett dragged his belongings from the back seat.

"Emmett, why are you taking all that stuff with you?"

"This is where we will be staying."

I looked around to neighboring hills, cacti and an occasional hawk on the wing. It was 11:30 and 100 degrees hot. I saw no convention center.

Emmett set his little suitcase on the concrete and began pulling it toward the closest glass structure.

I pulled my suitcase over to where Emmett stood with a small group of travelers.

Glass doors opened automatically, we entered and suddenly the carpeted floor moved downward until we reached a landing. Another set of doors opened. We briefly viewed a string of storefronts as a young couple moved into the elevator and settled against the side wall near Emmett.

The doors closed, we dropped to the next floor and stepped out onto a plush, green carpeted room half the size of a football field. Four rows of giant crystal light fixtures bloomed from the twelve-foot ceiling. Walls smothered in a silky beige fabric wrapped the room in opulence. At the far end of the hall, a large stage and podium peeked out from parted black velvet curtains. Above the stage was an imposing sign: The Roadrunner Room.

Portable wall partitions divided the giant room like a honeycomb alive with worker-bees mingling and setting up their cuckoo clock displays. Cuckoos spoke up every other second from every direction. In the center of the tick-tock chaos, a circle of four curved sofas created a social circle. Young women wearing green dresses and ruffled white aprons carried steins of beer to their customers lounging on the beige brocade sofas.

"So there really is a cuckoo clock convention."

"Yes, this is the main event," Emmett said, stepping back into the elevator. "I think you will enjoy the gift shops too. Hilda always did."

I followed him back inside the elevator.

Emmett pushed a button, the doors closed and we moved down another floor.

The doors dinged open to a long hallway with plush purple carpet and numbered doors on either side, just like an up-scale hotel. Emmett pulled out a card key and opened the door to number 312.

The spacious and well appointed room smelled like Lysol.

"Smells in here. I'll just open a window." I looked around.

"Sorry, Josephine, there are no windows. We're inside a mountain. This is your room and I'm right next door in 314. I'll put my things away and meet you here in half an hour." Emmett opened an inner door leading from my room to his.

"I feel claustrophobic without a window."

"I'm sorry, Josephine, it is what it is."

"Don't lock the door, Hooley. I want to be able to check on you if I need to. Are you sure there aren't any…?"

Windows?" He nodded and disappeared into the adjacent room.

I sat on my king-size bed, gave it a couple bounces and then the ultimate test. I kicked off my sandals and stretched out on the spread, feeling the firm but soft mattress under my tired body. The Lysol smell drifted away along with everything else.

Noise from the hallway woke me. It sounded like, "Har, har, yeah man," and some back slapping. I looked at the clock and then at the open door to Emmett's room. I rubbed my eyes, raced through the doorway and called his name. I even looked under his bed. I had turned my back for less than an hour and Hooley was gone.

CHAPTER ELEVEN

After a lot of walking and under-the-breath cursing, I finally found Emmett sitting at one of about fifty tables-for-four along the west wall of the Roadrunner Room. The twins from the airplane ride sat on either side of my friend. They had rosy complexions, hearty laughs and their bouncy bleached hair was canary yellow. Their plates were piled high with offerings from a string of side tables loaded with food and drink.

I pulled out the fourth chair and sat down.

Emmett made introductions and recommended the wienerwurst and deviled eggs.

Breakfast had been eight hours earlier and I was starving. I walked through the maze of diners to an impressive buffet, and helped myself. On my way back to Emmett's table I was so busy balancing my plate, trying to keep gravy from dripping on the floor that I didn't notice much else. Finally I became aware of Emmett, sitting alone, chin on chest.

"Hooley, Hooley!! Wake up. What's wrong, Emmett?" I dropped my plate on the table and lifted the old man's chin.

Emmett snorted some air and looked around.

"You scared me to death, Hooley! Who gave you this glass of wine?"

"Guess I fell asleep, Josephine. Old men do that."

"Ok, sorry…it's just that one minute you're chatting with the ladies and the next minute you're conked out. Where did your friends go?"

Emmett looked around and shrugged.

I scanned the convention center. A woman wearing a bun on her head caught my eye. I pointed to the plump woman dolled-up in a ruffled white blouse tucked into gray silky slacks. She stood about five yards from our table, working the coffee machine.

Hooley called her name.

Gertrude looked over her shoulder, smiled and rambled over to our table carrying a coffee mug and a giant helping of German chocolate cake. She wedged herself into a chair next to Emmett and quickly stuffed two blocks of cake into her mouth before she tried to speak. Chocolate crumbs came to rest amongst the ruffles. She finally looked at Emmett with chocolate-love still in her eyes.

"My dear Emmett, I wondered if you would be here…considering…ah, what happened to your dear sister." She shoved more cake into her mouth.

"Hilda would have wanted me to come," he smiled. "Did you come alone?"

"Not exactly." She glanced toward the stage. "A friend of mine is here. I had no idea he had plans to be here," she stuttered. "It seems Mr. Harburg is working security."

"Arnie's here?"

Gertrude nodded and changed the subject. She pointed to her sister's booth and invited us to see her collection of antique cuckoo clocks from Germany. She yammered on about eight-day tudor and eight-day chalet cuckoo clocks and a special twelve-day Black Forest cuckoo something-or-other with a Saint Bernard. Gertrude's sister specialized in antique clocks while most of the venders displayed clocks they'd made themselves, featuring all kinds of moving parts including people and animals coming and going, not to mention all kinds of cuckoo noise.

Even though I was familiar with Emmett and Hilda's creations, I was fascinated with the antique clocks on display. From there, Emmett led me all over the Roadrunner Room for the next two hours, inspecting clocks and chatting with their creators. He knew many of the makers and cuckoo connoisseurs in the room. They seemed to enjoy talking "clocks" with Mr. Hooley, the gentleman with endless knowledge and charm. When the knowledge and charm diminished, we decided to go to our rooms for a short rest.

We stuffed ourselves into the elevator along with a dozen other people. Some were just arriving with their suitcases. The convention was in full swing and noisier than feeding time at the zoo. The elevator stopped, the door dinged open and we walked down the hall to my room. I used the door key and watched Emmett enter his room from the connecting doorway.

I sat on the edge of my bed, head pounding to the beat of a million cuckoos.

Emmett stretched out on his bed and fell asleep immediately.

I wasn't at all sleepy so I slipped the door key back in my pocket, closed the door and headed for the elevator. The lift had a full load of people and the doors were closing. I squeezed into the overloaded cubicle, finally realizing how fully loaded it really was. My shoulder pressed against a large man's gut and a woman's purse was buried in my spine. Essence of tobacco, Jade East, BO and Corn Nuts permeated the public oxygen. The public groaned—or was it the elevator.

I figured everyone would be going up. I figured wrong. The muscular garlic breathing giant I was pressed up against pushed his finger on button B. After a fast drop, we lurched to a stop and the doors dinged opened. The huge maintenance man popped me out the doors like the pop of a waist button after dinner at Smorgy's.

I steadied myself against a stack of boxes labeled "Lysol" and turned back to the elevator, ready to hop a ride upstairs. But the doors had already closed.

Mr. Garlic was heading toward a set of open doors big enough for a large delivery truck to pass through. Feeling a bit claustrophobic, I decided to grab a little fresh air before I tried the elevator again. The closer I came to the over-sized door, the hotter I felt.

The outside air was burning hot but the view was interesting. An American flag fluttered weakly in the dry air above me. Below the flag, a windy road headed south. Black Canyon City sweltered in the distance. I walked to the edge of the concrete loading area and looked straight down about five-hundred yards to the wash, a wide, flat sandy area that would turn into a rushing, raging river whenever flash-floods happened. I wished for a monsoon as sweat poured down my face.

Off to my right, a delivery truck was grinding its way up the road. To my left there were stacks of boxes filled with fruits and vegetables from California.

Mr. Garlic paid no attention to me, hefted a stack of boxes onto a dolly and pushed it inside the building.

I heard a rustling sound near my foot and what sounded like a meow. I looked down.

Something moved inside an open cardboard box decorated with pictures of avocados.

I leaned closer.

A little fury critter cowering in one corner of the box moved its eyes up to meet mine. Three paws were tangled in green plastic mesh used in the packing of produce such as avocados. The fourth paw tore wildly at the constraints.

I heard another meow and leaned closer, but the roar of a motor made it impossible to hear anything else. I sat on the heels of my sandals and peeked under a flap of cardboard. Just as I touched the box, the deafening roar of a delivery truck startled me. The truck began to slow and turn toward the open doors of the hotel. I felt heat from the engine and leaned forward over the box, dodging the giant tires as they made the turn.

I teetered from toes to heels a couple times, lost my balance and followed the box over the side of the mountain.

Desperate meows and falling rocks were all I heard. I rolled a few feet on hard ground before I was able to grab onto something solid. Unfortunately the cactus was not a good choice. Needles penetrated my right hand as my left hand reached out for the yowling box. I gripped the cardboard but instantly let go of the cactus.

Hugging the rocky bank, heart pounding in my ears, I wiggled my body into a vertical position and pulled one leg up. My foot found a rock I thought I could trust, but the rock cut loose and rolled down the mountain, taking hundreds of little rocks with it. I opened my mouth to yell for help, but sand filled my mouth as more rocks headed south with me in the lead. I hung onto the box as I slid on my side, faster and faster. Dust and sand showered my head. Rocks under foot loosened, rolled and clattered all the way down to the wash.

It was not by choice that I found another cactus. I brushed by the prickly brute, adding needles to the bruises up and down my side. As my body leaned, I began to roll again. I reached out, desperately trying to find something to grab hold of. I don't remember letting go of the box but I do remember watching it skittle over the falling cascade of debris below me.

My last thoughts were like clouds slipping over the horizon. It was hard to think clearly while falling at high speeds, inhaling dust and coughing my brains out. I remember the pain every time I grazed another rock or slid by another poky cactus. My last thought was, "I probably murdered the poor kitten," and then the lights went out. Not that the lights ever go out in Arizona during daylight hours. But my lights were definitely out.

Everything was dark when I finally opened my eyes. My fuzzy brain thought I'd gone blind until I turned my head and saw stars sprinkled against an inky sky. My neck felt stiff when I tried to raise my head so I lay still thinking about the cool air, hard ground and total quiet. I didn't remember being in Arizona until I heard a faint little meow. Slowly the convention center, the kitten and the delivery truck came back to me.

When I tried to sit up, an avalanche of sand and pebbles poured off my aching body. I pushed more dirt and debris off my legs. One leg screamed with pain. I ran a hand down to my right ankle. It felt hotter and fatter than the left one.

I heard another soft meow, forgot about my ankle and reached in the direction of the sound. All I felt was sand. I crawled a few yards. My waving arm finally connected with the box. I pulled it closer to me and reached inside. Sharp little teeth clamped down on my hand but did not break the skin.

"Now be good, little kitty," I cooed. "Nice little kitty…I'm going to help you. Ouch!"

I reached into the box. Using both hands, I pulled at the plastic mesh with all my strength until the threads began to break. I pulled again and again until the whole mess came loose and the kitten was free. I lifted the little guy out of the box and put him against my belly. His breathing slowed as he relaxed and we quickly fell asleep on hard ground under a moonless sky.

Some time later, my eyes popped open when I heard a coyote howl. The howl seemed to come from behind me. I held onto the kitty and stood up. Crazy thoughts raced through my head. *Do coyotes run in packs? Do they eat little kittens or wounded women?* These thoughts pushed me forward on rough ground in utter darkness. Hobbling along, I imagined hearing a bat and then an owl. The coyote howled again as another winged creature flapped cool air across my face. Fear was the engine behind my trek across the desert.

A pink tinge grew on the horizon, lighting up the desert enough for me to see that I was severely lost. Day time fears replaced my fear of the dark, coyotes, rattle snakes and huge spiders. When my energy was completely spent, I collapsed on the ground, hugging the kitty. I thought about David. *Would he miss me? Would Mom and Dad cry? Would vultures clean my bones?*

Sometime later, I opened my eyes and looked around—wondering if I'd dreamt the fall down the mountain and the painful walk in the dark. I was lying on an Indian blanket on the dirt floor of a cool shaded place that looked like someone's home. It smelled like a campfire, looked like a cave and had a Safeway shopping cart parked in the living room. I looked around for my little kitten.

"Lady, don't move. I need to pull the spines out," a woman's voice told me.

I turned my head and looked into a pair of serious eyes—one brown, one blue.

The tall, brown-skinned woman held my shoulder down with one hand, clamped her pliers onto a cactus spine and yanked. Even as I cried out in pain, she went for the next and the next. Some of the stickers were broken and took several tries before they'd give up the flesh. She told me to roll over and then she yanked more cactus spines from my backside. Despite my pathetic whimpering, she never faltered with those terrible pliers. Then came the hot compresses followed by an oily smelly salve. Her brown eye twitched, but the blue one stayed focused on her victim until every swollen hurting spot had a coat of salve covering it.

"Thank you, ah …I think I feel better, sort of."

"You'll feel better tomorrow," she said with a swish of her long black ponytail, and walked away.

I closed my eyes, wishing I was unconscious. Any movement brought more pain—especially in the ankle. I cringed when I saw the woman walking toward me carrying a bucket of water and a washcloth. She washed and dried my foot, came back with a roll of stretchy cloth-wrap and what looked like a large black boot.

"Where did you get all this stuff?" I asked.

"The store." She could have said, "The store, stupid," but she didn't. "Actually, I wrenched my foot last fall. I had to make a brace out of kitchen utensils and wrap it with saran wrap. I hobbled all the way to Black Canyon City for help. The Doc sold me this boot and I stocked up on medical supplies in case I hurt myself again."

"You don't have a car?"

"I don't have a road," she grinned.

As soon as my foot was expertly wrapped, the young woman slipped the open boot into place, closed it around my ankle and secured it with Velcro straps. She grabbed my hand and told me to stand up.

"You've got to be kidding...I mean, wow, I'm standing. Not too bad. The boot takes all the pressure off my foot. This is great. Thank you."

"Name's Dee; what's yours?"

"Josephine Stuart. It's nice to meet you Dee. Is this your home?"

Her brown eye twitched when she told me she'd lived in the cave for almost one year. She said she was a college student and came to Arizona to study javalinas, wild burros and bobcats for a book she was working on. Her blue eye teared up when she said she'd wanted to get away from the rat race of the Bay Area, and besides, her boyfriend had left her for another woman.

Dee deftly fingered her hair into a tighter ponytail and reapplied the rubber band.

I finally became aware of what a mess I was. My nicest linen summer outfit was shredded and filthy. The baby blue calf-length pants were ruined. A chunk of sleeve from the matching top hung over my arm like a ripe scab. I hadn't looked in a mirror yet, but I knew I was filthy—except for the areas where Dee had dressed my wounds.

"May I ask what you were doing lying in the gully holding a bobcat in your arms?"

"A what?" I stammered, bracing myself against the cool clay wall. "Are you sure it was a bobcat?"

"Very sure. I presented the little fellow to his mother this morning and then carried you here."

"And where is, here?"

"A bit of a hike from where I found you. I was collecting hair specimens—part of my research on a family of bobcats."

I explained how I'd fallen down the mountain, tried to find my way in the dark and fell asleep holding a bobcat in my arms. I listened to my own voice and thought I sounded like a crazy woman, but Dee nodded her head as if people and bobcats fell out of mountains everyday. I had the sense that even though Dee seemed to be bitter towards the general population of the world, I was OK because I rescued a bobcat.

Fortunately, Dee's one room abode stayed cool all day. She heated a pot of water over a small campfire and reconstituted a packet of dehydrated soup for our lunch. After lunch she handed me a cup of tea. Something she concocted for pain.

The outside world sizzled in the mid-day sun while we relaxed in comfort. Dee wrote in her log for hours while I sat on a colorful blanket staring at various stalactite formations on the ceiling. Later we shared more information about ourselves, some girl-talk and a few giggles.

Dee went back to her writing and I watched a drop of water run to the end of a stalactite and drop with a ping into a cooking pot positioned two feet from my head. I entertained myself by counting the seconds between drops. By my watch, the pot pinged every thirteen seconds.

I dozed off for a while, until Dee shook my shoulder.

"Josephine, you were having a nightmare."

"Yeah, Hooley was in trouble and I couldn't help him because my foot was in a bear trap."

"We should be going now," she said. "It'll be dark in a couple hours."

"Ah, yeah, I really need to get back. Emmett's probably out of his mind worrying about me. But do you know how to get to the flat-topped mountain?" I asked, noticing that Dee had changed into clean shorts and t-shirt.

"Once we get out in the open, away from the cave, look that way. It's a few miles east of here. I think it's closer than going to Black Canyon City. I packed up my notes, a little food and some clothes. I'm going with you back to the Bay Area." She swung a fully stuffed backpack over her shoulder.

Dee didn't ask me if she could go home with us. She just said she was going. But that was OK because I owed her a lot and was glad to help her out. She slipped a duffle bag over my arm. I teetered, found my balance and joined her outside. The sun was a ball of red fire at our backs, ready to drop behind a mountain contoured like the Indian head on an old nickel.

Dee marched with enthusiasm in her hiking boots and headphones, never looking back.

I thunked along behind, my aching body struggling to keep pace as I swerved around cacti and large rocks where I imagined tarantulas and snakes were hiding from the blazing sun. The big black boot worked out better than I'd have imagined. It was the one part of my body protected from snakes and cactus spines. Looking ahead, I recognized a bump on the horizon as the flat-top mountain. Looking over my right shoulder, I saw Black Canyon City with its clusters of little red roofs and small patches of green spread over gently rolling hills, several miles south of Dee's cave.

An hour passed, the sun disappeared and the temperature plummeted into double digits. I felt refreshed, even hopeful. We had such a long way to go and my ankle felt like it was broken in five places. The cooler air cooled even more. I sat on a tarantula rock and shook the sand out of my sandals.

Dee must have sensed I was not around and looked back. She sat on a rock and waited for me. By the time I caught up, the sky had turned from red to purple and would soon be black. Half an hour later, we could not see our destination, but Dee seemed confident on the path she chose. I followed close behind her, keeping an eye out for cougars and coyotes.

Dee told me we were close to a family of burros. I couldn't see them, but I heard their breath, felt their heat and smelled their musty odor. I wished we could hop on their backs and ride up to the mountain. Dee talked about various families of burros, especially her favorite—Bob, Barb and Bear. She told me not to worry about bobcats and to be on the lookout for javelinas—pig-like animals related to the hippopotamus. I gulped at the thought of a hippo-sized pig. She assured me they were smaller than hippos.

I found out Dee was one semester short of a Masters and one animal species short of a full book. She planned to study the eating habits of the raccoon when she got back to California. I told her about the ones in my neighborhood who were not finicky eaters. They liked Italian, Mexican and Chinese best—straight out of the garbage can.

We chatted about our lives for another hour as we cautiously made our way over desert fraught with dangerous animals and poky cactus spines.

I told Dee that all men were not like her ex-boyfriend. I told her about David—his good looks, his sense of humor and his thoughtfulness. I don't know if Dee was even listening, but my little speech brought tears to my eyes.

CHAPTER TWELVE

Tiny headlights appeared on the horizon.

Dee and I cast long shadows on pavement leading up to the barely visible flat-top mountain less than a mile away. She waved her arms. I yawned. My imagination had already jumped ahead to a comfortable seat, a ride up the hill and a quick elevator trip to my bed. I smiled in the dark and let go of a few knots in my neck.

"Kind of sounds like a truck," Dee said. "That's a good thing. They're more likely to stop."

Seconds later a white delivery van idled two feet away. The driver motioned for us to jump in so we crammed ourselves into the one bucket seat available. My shoulder pressed against the door while Dee's shoulder rubbed against the driver's large frame. The man wore a blue uniform and his profile looked familiar.

"Do I know you from somewhere?" I asked.

"Are you girls making a pass at me?" he grinned in the green light from the dash.

"Yeah, we do that whenever we get lost in the desert and lose our minds," Dee said.

Ten silent minutes and a twisty ride later, the van pulled to a stop and we piled out. Two spotlights shone down from either side of two giant metal doors ensconced in the hillside. I remembered standing on that same loading platform and hearing the cry of a kitten I named Buster.

"The doors are closed," Dee said. "How do we get in?"

"Yeah, we should have taken the other road," I said.

"I should have let you broads walk," he grunted, and tooted the horn. A minute later the metal doors parted and he parked the van inside.

I studied the man's face for half a second in the light and knew he was Arnie from the Watsonville bank, but said nothing.

"You gals can help me unload and then I'll show you how to use the off-hours elevator."

We dropped our packs on the concrete floor and followed Arnie to the back of the van. He opened the doors, revealing five flat wooden crates, each about four feet by three feet.

Dee grabbed one corner and I got the other. We walked a heavy crate over to a side of the building where similar crates were stacked ten high. Before letting go, I tried to see what was inside.

"Hey! What do you think you're doing?" Arnie shouted.

We walked back to the van for another crate.

Arnie shoved a second box out the back end of the van and Dee and I hauled it over to the designated spot.

"Who does he think he is…?" Dee muttered.

By the fifth crate we were ready to ring the man's neck. Lucky for him, he finally punched in a code next to the elevator and it dinged open. I pressed the three-button and felt around in my pockets for my room key.

"Looking for your key?" Dee asked, pulling a card key from her pocket. "I found this. When you told me you were staying at the convention center, I knew you were telling me the truth."

"So why wouldn't I tell you the truth?"

"Sometimes people don't...."

The door dinged open. We found room 314 and Dee stuck the room-card in the door slot.

I pushed the door open and flipped on a light.

Someone groaned across the room.

"Who's sleeping in my bed?" I snapped.

The lumpy bed moved and two heads full of springy bleached blond hair popped up in surprise. They looked at us with blinking eyes as if we were space creatures invading their domicile. Actually, the two mops of hair springing out in all directions looked very spacy.

"OK, ladies, time to leave," Dee said, in a take-charge voice.

Clad only in their underwear, the women quickly dressed and flew out the door.

Emmett stumbled over to the doorway of his connecting room wearing forty-niner shorts, a t-shirt and a surprised look on his face.

I asked Hooley if he was OK. He smiled and squeezed my hand, the one with acute cactus pain.

Tears came to my eyes.

Hooley looked touched. He said he'd looked everywhere for me. The twins had felt sorry for him and followed him to his room. He guessed they had settled in for the night. As he spoke, his eyebrows came together.

"What's the matter, Hooley?"

"Pardon me, Josephine, but you look like you just came out of a sandstorm."

"Pretty good guess. Emmett, I'd like you to meet my friend, Dee Morales. She saved my life and brought me here."

Dee and Emmett shook hands. She told him the full story of my disappearance while I silently sang in the shower. A ton of sand, worry and pain swirled down the drain.

When I finally finished my shower and stepped out of the bathroom, Emmett was snoring in his room and Dee was in my room sound asleep on the carpet with the bedspread pulled up around her. I guessed she would need time to adjust to civilization after a whole year of sleeping on a rug in a cave. At least it was a furnished cave inhabited by previous students studying various aspects of the desert. But not furnished enough for my taste.

After four hours of dead-to-the-world sleep, my eyes opened and my mind raced. It was five o'clock in the morning. I stared at the ceiling asking myself, why were Gertrude and Arnie at the convention center? And the crated paintings, why were they downstairs stacked up against the wall? Why was Arnie delivering at night and why did he know how to operate the outside doors and the elevator? Our recent hitch-hike ride up the mountain reminded me of the day Emmett did some banking in Watsonville. Arnie worked at the bank that day and a few minutes later parked next to us at the pharmacy several blocks away. Too many coincidences!

I dressed quietly in the dark, pulled on the black boot and snuck out the door. I took the empty elevator to the basement and looked around the well-lit warehouse. Hotel employees wheeled boxes of food ingredients into freight elevators while maids filled their carts with fresh linen and cleaning supplies. In all the hustle-bustle, I figured no one would pay attention to me as I discreetly thunked over to the crates Arnie had delivered the night before. I picked at a piece of the wood cover I thought was extra thin. A large sliver broke off and part of that lodged itself under my fingernail. It hurt, but nothing compared to cactus spines.

I felt eyes on my back and whipped my head around to see if anyone was watching me.

"Ma'am, do you have business down here?" a short woman wearing a maid outfit asked.

"Actually …I was, ah, looking for something…."

"I'm sorry, Ma'am, this floor is for employees only." She turned and walked away.

I took a quick look at the small spot of canvas I'd uncovered. It was definitely a painting. I saw a couple scribbled black letters of the artist's name on a background of red paint the size of my throbbing finger. A doctor's signature would have been more legible.

I left the basement and snuck back into my room. Lying in bed, I wished for a window with a view of the sunrise. I imagined seeing a sunrise, a burro, a javelina and a baby bobcat named Buster. Sweet little Buster.

Suddenly my cell phone played Beethoven's Fifth. I leaped out of bed, barely missing Dee's head as she turned toward the loud music. I grabbed the phone from my purse, listened to the familiar voice and smiled. David said he'd called Sunday, but Emmett couldn't find me. He thought I'd call back as soon as I could and when I didn't he began to worry.

"Hi, David, we're having a great time…."

"I'm glad. I started to worry when you didn't call back. Guess you were too busy."

"Yes, I was busy and I wasn't near a phone. I was in a cave in the desert…I'll tell you all about it when I get home."

"Huh? OK, Josie. I'll talk to you later, when you're more awake."

"I'm awake. Thanks for calling, David." We hung up.

Dee stepped out of the bathroom looking clean and refreshed, not to mention beautiful.

Half an hour later, the three of us rode the elevator up to an elaborate breakfast buffet.

Gertrude saw us coming and pointed to the end of the line.

The bobble-head twins arrived, giggling as they queued up behind us.

After breakfast, Emmett asked me to drive him to Black Canyon City.

Feeling like a claustrophobic mole, I was more than happy to drive the jeep into town.

Hooley sat in the back seat and Dee rode shotgun with her window down. The fresh desert air was in the low eighties, heading toward triple digits. We saw very few cars on the road. No Monday morning commute to worry about, just sand and cacti, sand and more cacti until five black SUVs bearing little green flags roared by us, heading for the flat-top mountain.

"What was that?"

"The flag is from Saudi Arabia," Dee said.

Emmett concurred.

It was exactly ten o'clock when we arrived in Black Canyon City. Emmett directed us to a library even smaller than the one in Aromas. I parked at the curb and watched an elderly woman unlock the front door. She turned and waved madly at Emmett as he climbed out of the jeep.

"You girls go have some fun. You can pick me up at eleven," he said, waving us on.

The jeep idled while Dee and I watched the woman give Emmett a hug before he stepped inside the building. Either this was a very friendly town or

Hooley had a history with the librarian. I smiled at the thought.

We decided to stop at the local diner for an iced tea. The breakfast rush, if there was one, was obviously over and lunch hadn't started, giving us peace and quiet. I told Dee about some of the murals I had painted over the years and she told me about her hikes to the top of various famous mountains including last year's trip to Mount Kilimanjaro where she met a special gentleman. She fell silent for a moment of reflection.

"Dee, you said you were living in the bay area. Where does your family come from originally?"

"I'm going to Stanford, but my family is from Mexico."

"My best friend, Alicia, is from Tijuana. She's about your size and her hair is jet black like yours."

"I bet she doesn't have one blue eye."

"Well, no...."

Dee asked how I knew Emmett and I ended up telling her the whole sad story. "Oh, no, it's already eleven-thirty," I said as I dropped money on the table and we hurried to the jeep.

"I don't know why we should be in a rush to pick him up," Dee said. "Maybe he'd like more time with his friend."

I parked at the curb in front of the library and we waited for Emmett.

"Look, she walked him to the door. I don't see any books. Do you?" I asked.

"No, of course not. What's he going to do, return them next year?"

Dee had a point.

Emmett climbed in and closed the door.

"Well, Hooley, we're dying to know. Who she is?"

"Mrs. Crane is just an old friend. She was so excited. She told me that a Prince and his entourage from Saudi Arabia passed through town this morning. She said they passed by her house. She couldn't stop talking about it—until I told her about Hilda."

On the way back to the hotel, Dee was unusually quiet as she stared out her window.

Emmett told us about an international art auction scheduled to begin at nine o'clock in the evening at the hotel convention center. He said that he and Hilda always stayed at the hotel an extra day to enjoy the "invitation only sale." He said he used to bid on pieces of jewelry and antique clocks to sell in his jewelry stores.

My imagination suddenly turned Emmett's clock shops into Tiffany stores featuring plush red carpet and giant crystal chandeliers.

As we rolled through town, Emmett pointed out the fire department, grocery store, elementary school and post office. Black Canyon City was four blocks long, twice as big as Aromas.

"Last fall, your friend Mrs. Crane gave me a ride to the doctor," Dee said. "I strapped a spatula and a wooden spoon onto my ankle with saran wrap and walked all the way to Highway 17 with a chipped bone in my foot. She drove me the last mile."

"She's a fine woman." He smiled. "Very fine."

We motored straight into the desert on the long hot strip of blacktop stretching north. There were very few cars on the road. Most were going south, heading toward Black Canyon City, Phoenix and beyond.

I parked the jeep on top of the flat-top mountain and looked around at clusters of fine cars. A Rolls idled in the space next to us. It went silent and four Armani suits climbed out. The distinctive black SUVs with green flags were lined up on the east side of the parking lot. A caravan of three white Mercedes and a very old Jaguar chose the west side. More luxury cars funneled into the parking lot as the hoi polloi streamed out, taking their cuckoos with them.

CHAPTER THIRTEEN

Our hotel sizzled with excitement. There was hardly a cuckoo left in the Roadrunner Room. On the stage behind black velvet curtains, preparations were being made for the auction. Precious cargo was wheeled in and set up for the grand event, but we had to use our imaginations because the curtains were closed. I did manage to peek into the area for a moment before a workman told me to get lost.

Dee wasn't nearly as excited about the auction as I was because she'd found an old friend—her friend from the Mount Kilamanjaro hike. He happened to be a Prince, the youngest son of Arabian royalty and looked like a young Gregory Peck with a goatee. In mere moments Dee's tough exterior had melted, exposing a softer, sweeter, more feminine side, more like a flirtatious innocent teenager. She introduced Emmett and me to the handsome Prince who wore Nike's with his grey silk suit. We didn't see them again until the auction started at nine.

Dee invited us to sit with her and the Prince in the first row.

I was thrilled, but Gertrude and the twins had already saved Emmett a seat in the back row. I heard giggling and looked over my shoulder. Emmett had lipstick on his cheek and a splash of wine on his white shirt. He was anything but unhappy. I was happy that Emmett had packed his new white shirt and grey slacks and wished I'd done as well for myself. My short black skirt and rust color blouse that matched my hair would have to do. The black boot coordinated nicely with my skirt but not with my white sandal. A last minute gift shop purchase of a long black silk scarf added a nice touch.

I looked around the room and saw nothing but opulence, women wearing jewelry I'd only seen in magazine advertisements. A few of the older men wore tuxedos but not the Prince. He looked like a bit of a rebel in his day suit, and Nikes. Everyone in his entourage was dressed to perfection.

Dee looked exotic with her hair stacked on top of her head, held in place by a silver cord. Her black sleeveless jumpsuit was the perfect backdrop for a silver and turquoise squash blossom necklace I'd admired in the gift shop earlier.

The curtains parted, the auctioneer was introduced and the sale began. The first item for sale was an antique clock from Bulgaria. I looked over my shoulder at Emmett to see what he thought of the clock. Emmett didn't see the clock because the gals were busy trying to clean the stain off his shirt. But I did see a couple late arrivals who happened to be my friends, the Halikiases. Irene waved her fingers at me from her third row seat.

I returned the wave, and turned back to the auctioneer as he unveiled a painting where blue squiggly worms or spaghetti crawled over the large canvas. After Pollock came paintings by Vermeer, Hopper, Boccioni and Russo.

After a two-minute break, the auctioneer held up a diamond necklace. I looked over my shoulder to see Emmett's reaction. His eyes looked droopy as he rested his head on Gertrude's shoulder. He obviously was not interested in the necklace. But the Prince was interested and after some back and forth bidding, won the bid. Dee contained her excitement but I sensed she was bursting at the seams. Was the necklace meant for her?

Next came a bust of Eisenhower, several Impressionist paintings and more jewelry. The bidding was robust, but the excitement and enthusiasm was not enough to keep me from yawning. It was late and I was tired. I wondered how Emmett was doing. I looked back at the last row and four empty chairs. I figured the gals were looking after him and had put him to bed. I decided to stay a little while longer.

More clocks, jewelry and a statue of Cleopatra were sold off and another round of paintings was presented. A painting by Roy Miller took me by surprise—an ugly surprise actually. The nonsensical slashes of dark colors reminded me of some of the paintings at the Halikias Gallery back home. I glanced back at Irene and Nico. They were beaming. I guessed Roy was their boy.

To my great surprise, people actually seemed to like Roy's painting. The bidding was intense and the painting eventually sold for gobs of money. I was astonished to see the Prince pay $230,000.

Dee turned her head and whispered, "the Prince already has one of Roy's paintings at home in the palace. If you ask me, that's the only reason they're valuable now."

I didn't think much of the Prince's art choices but he and Dee made a handsome couple and I was happy for her.

I decided to leave them and check on Emmett. I took the elevator to my room, peeked in on the old man, changed into a big t-shirt and climbed into my bed.

Tuesday morning, Emmett and I met up with Dee and the Prince over breakfast. I expected to see Gertrude and the twins but they weren't around. Dee told us she'd be leaving with the Prince on a trip to Peru. The news didn't surprise me. Why go home and write a book when she could be climbing mountains with a real hunk like the Prince? I wished them well and thanked Dee for helping me out of the desert. We exchanged e-mail addresses and promised to keep in touch.

Irene and Nico joined us at the breakfast buffet. Their share from the sale of Roy's paintings was a substantial amount and Nico was in an unusually good mood, bragging about how he'd taken advice from a friend and invested in "his boy Roy."

I swear I saw dollar signs in Nico's eyeballs.

Dee said her last goodbyes and excused herself from the table to join the Prince and his entourage.

Irene and Nico gulped the last of their coffee and headed back to their rooms to pack.

Emmett and I hauled our luggage to the Jeep and took off for Phoenix Sky Harbor Airport, a forty-minute drive from Black Canyon City.

"Emmett why didn't you stay for the rest of the auction last night?"

"I wanted to but the girls had other ideas. Gertrude said the stain on my shirt looked bad and I should change. The twins were feeling restless and I don't think they cared about the auction so we took a walk to my room, planning to come back later, but I fell asleep. Might have been the wine."

"So where did the wine come from?"

"Gertrude had a bottle in that big leather bag she carries. She made several toasts to friendship and clock making and the convention and yada yada yada."

"Oh, well, you didn't miss anything at the auction. About the time you left, they brought out some pretty ugly stuff," I said as I parked the Jeep at the rental agency. We dragged our luggage two blocks to the bus stop and climbed aboard a free shuttle to Southwest Airlines. If the airport grew any bigger it would be a major city. Poor Emmett was still trying to catch his breath when the bus stopped and the driver tossed our luggage to the curb.

I asked Emmett if I could push him in a wheelchair but he didn't like the idea. He planned to walk to the gate the same as he did every other year. In his mind, it wasn't so much that he was getting older, it was all about the airport getting bigger. By the time we limped up to Gate 23, we were the last to board. The twins had saved a seat for the old man and I got stuck with an isle seat at the rear, my boot resting in the aisle.

Sunny skies greeted us at the San Jose airport. We deplaned and walked the required distance, grabbed our luggage off the turnstile and hustled out to the sidewalk. A rush of cold air pushed us toward the shuttle bus. We boarded and jiggled and swayed, shoulder to shoulder, with a full load of passengers to the parking lot. I spotted the truck. We hobbled up to it, climbed aboard and headed west into the afternoon commute.

California was still in its greenest season. After my desert experience, it looked greener than ever. Aromas looked like a scene from Austria with its emerald hills, trees and quaint buildings. Home looked good too, especially the yellow ribbon David tied to the front door. He missed me. I'd missed him too and there he was standing in the doorway with Solow at his side. Solow galloped up to me, howling with glee.

David met me halfway with a big hug and a short but passionate kiss.

Emmett caught up to us, shook hands with David and rolled his luggage into the house.

"Josie, what's with the boot?" David asked.

It took the rest of the afternoon for me to answer and explain and talk about all the things that had happened in the last four days. David periodically locked eyes with Emmett who nodded his head, validating my explanations. David still looked a little confused, but I was tired of explanations. Instead, I brought out iced tea and peanut butter cookies for everyone.

"So David, was there any excitement around here while we were gone?"

"Almost got run over by a white van this morning," he laughed.

"Really?" I felt the hairs on the back of my neck raise up. I told myself not to be oversensitive when it came to white vans. There were millions of white vans in the world.

"What do you mean David? What kind of white van? You mean like a delivery van?"

"I don't know...it was white and it was a van; I didn't pay much attention to details. I was too busy getting out of his way. This sounds crazy but this guy jumped out of the van, picked up your newspaper, jumped back in and took off down the road, just missing me and Solow. I'm starting to sound like you, sweetie," he laughed.

"So what did the guy look like?"

"I don't know. He was kind of tall, lanky, wore a red baseball cap—backwards, of course. That's about it."

"Old enough to know better?" I scratched my head.

"Yeah, plenty old enough. Don't worry, I'll bring my paper over for you."

"A person would have to be pretty desperate to steal newspapers. It's not the newspaper I'm worried about, but sure, I'd like to read it. Thanks, David."

David said he'd bring the paper over later. First he wanted me to try his new recipe for shrimp and spinach pizza.

Emmett and I were willing tasters—willing to be fed hot pizza comfort food after traveling all day. It felt good to travel once in a while, but Solow needed extra attention, comforting and bites of pizza, because of our time away from each other.

After dinner, Emmett trundled off to bed and David jogged down to his house for the newspaper, leaving me alone with the evening news and frozen peas on my ankle.

I was in a very relaxed state, kind of post-lobotomy, digesting dinner state of mind, when a story flashed on the screen that brought me to full attention. A perky young reporter talked about the newly-famous local artist, Roy Miller, hitting the big time at the international auction in Arizona. That story led to a quick shot of Dee, the Prince and his majesty's royally garish acquisition.

Ms. Perky was in full awe.

David arrived with the newspaper and tossed it on the kitchen table. We spent a lovely evening together making up for my time away. No more questions—no more explanations, just happiness being together.

I wished my dreams that night could have been as wonderful. Unfortunately, the last dream turned into a nightmare where little minivans were running over pigeons lined up as if in a bowling alley—feathers and black paint everywhere.

CHAPTER FOURTEEN

What a treat to wake up in my own bed in my own bedroom—not in a cave or a hotel room. I bounced out of bed, into the shower, into my clothes and into the kitchen for a hot cup of coffee. Emmett had something on his mind and wanted to talk. I told him I'd listen when I had time, like after work. He seemed to understand that work was on my mind, and I needed to hurry to get there on time. I hugged Hooley goodbye and gave Solow a doggie treat.

The Wednesday morning commute was light, the sun was out and the salty air was invigorating. I was ready for a day of painting with my friends, and they were ready for me to instruct them. The Parthenon looked too new. I told Alicia and Kyle to add a few cracks and dings to the exterior and demonstrated by creating a horizontal crack in one of the pillars.

Irene and Nico arrived at noon looking like disheveled travelers finally home from a quick trip to Arizona. The money glow was still on Nico's face. Irene examined the cracked pillar and nodded her head in approval.

"You're right, Josephine. The Parthenon needs a little aging. Wasn't that the most exciting auction you've ever been to? By the way, how's your ankle?"

"Actually, I forgot to wear the boot today. My ankle isn't hurting so I must be all right," I said. "To tell you the truth, I'd never been to an auction." I noticed Alicia's stare. "The best part of the trip was meeting Dee and the Prince."

Alicia's mouth dropped open.

Kyle's eyes were big.

Irene and Nico went to work inside the gallery, leaving me to explain about Dee, the Prince and the painting. I talked all the way through lunch and half of the afternoon, beginning with my fall from the delivery dock, two nights in the desert and twin bobble-heads taking care of Emmett. When I told Alicia about Dee Morales her eyes lit up. She told me her maiden name was Morales, a very common name, actually. She said that Trigger had been searching through lists of people with the Morales name but needed more information.

Around three o'clock, I decided to take a break with some iced tea and a look inside the gallery. Surprisingly, two of the four walls were almost filled with artwork and the glass display case held several large fused glass and hand blown glass pieces of stunning artwork. Nico stood near the top of an eight-foot ladder while Irene handed him a large framed collage by the famous Dorothy Helen. Half a dozen paintings rested against the wall waiting their turn to be hung. Five of them were Roy Miller creations.

Alicia came up behind me and whispered, "Jo, how much did Roy's painting sell for?"

"Over two-hundred thousand dollars." I rolled my eyes to the ceiling and Alicia grabbed her throat, pretending to choke. "It was a lot like this one over here." I pointed to a framed black and blue and red nightmare.

Alicia shook her head.

"My feelings exactly."

After two more hours of painting, we were ready to hit the road and deal with the traffic. Kyle had finished painting the roof tiles and Alicia had already begun work on the Greek figures just below the peak of the Parthenon's roof. Shading would give the figures a three dimensional look. I came in with the highlights. It was like carving into stone except with brushes, and when we were done, the façade would look more like stone than real stone.

I drove straight home, looking forward to an evening with my boys—Solow, David and Emmett.

The house was quiet. Two minutes after I arrived, David walked in with Solow on a leash and several pieces of mail stuck in his pocket.

"David, you two look exhausted. You went to Emmett Place?" I kept my eyes on the door to see if Emmett was going to join us.

"Yeah, we had quite an afternoon. Emmett put me to work watering the plants, trimming the fruit trees, raking leaves—you name it." He wiped his brow and handed me the mail.

"The way you're smiling, I think you had a good time over there and I'm sure that Solow had a wonderful time. So, where's Emmett?"

"About two-thirty, Rusty picked up Emmett and drove him to his dentist appointment." David took the leash off of Solow. "Keeping Lilly out of the rose bushes was my biggest job."

A moment later, we heard squealing brakes and a motor coughing itself quiet. Solow ran to the front door. It opened and Emmett, Rusty and Fahima entered the living room. Emmett flashed his new tooth smile at me while Rusty placed a bucket of fried chicken on the kitchen table.

Fahima grumbled and cursed as she pushed her large hips into my small rocking chair. She re-wrapped a black scarf tightly around her head, perfectly framing her saggy face. She refused to make eye contact and answered my friendly questions with grunts.

David and Rusty had taken over the kitchen chores. When it was all done, we had heaps of fried chicken arranged on a platter, a green salad the size of Rhode Island and two pitchers of iced tea. They called us to dinner with proud grins on their faces and red cheeks in Rusty's case.

Fahima made the first move to get up, but the rocking chair wouldn't let go.

Emmett saw her struggling and held the back of the chair while I took Fahima's cold hands and pulled her up. She rubbed her hips and growled something in another language. I don't think it was thank you. Two drumsticks and three wings later, her disposition had improved.

Emmett announced that his new tooth was working better than all of Rusty's teeth put together.

Rusty laughed. "I can do anything you can do, Emmett, only much better."

"How long have you two known each other?" David asked.

"Ever since Rusty's father rented out part of his shop to me," Emmett said, flashing his new tooth smile. "I was young but Rusty was just a kid. He liked to help me with the clocks. He was a good kid, always running errands for me."

Fahima listened with a furrowed brow, but mellowed a little when the ice cream was served. When David brought out the chocolate sauce, her lip twitched like she might even smile.

Solow was in high heaven, catching every dropped tidbit of food under the table. Lucky for him, old folk tend to drop things on a regular basis, especially Rusty who made sure that Solow was included in the feast.

"Look, Rusty," Emmett said, "the sun is almost down. It will be dark in half an hour."

"I didn't realize it was so late. I can't drive in the dark."

"Don't worry, Rusty, you can stay in my cottage tonight."

"Well, it wasn't too bad last time. What do you say Fahima?"

Fahima glared at Rusty—probably her way of saying, "if we must."

Our guests left the house, climbed into the Oldsmobile and backed down the driveway just before dark.

We didn't hear from Rusty and Fahima until ten minutes later when brakes squealed, pistons pounded to a stop, doors slammed and the odd couple burst into the living room without knocking—out of breath and shaken.

Rusty tried to explain, but his tongue was in a knot.

Fahima rattled on in her other language, periodically shrieking and flailing her arms. Finally, she crossed her arms over her chest, sucked in some air and told us in plain English that someone had trashed the cottage.

David's jaw dropped, Emmett looked pale and my heart thumped in my chest like a chimpanzee on the bongos.

"Did you see anyone?" David asked.

Looking white as a ghost, Rusty shook his toupee off center.

Emmett put an arm over his friend's shoulder while I helped Fahima into a chair, remembering too late the dimensions of the infamous rocker.

David suggested we call the police.

Emmett shook his head and groaned while Rusty paced the floor.

I took a deep breath, assessed the situation, suggesting we wait until morning to take action.

David frowned. "How do you know these thugs won't come back and do more damage?"

"They were obviously looking for something," I said. "If they found it, they won't be back. If they didn't find it, they won't be back tonight."

David shrugged and offered his guest bedroom to Rusty and Fahima. They were quick to take him up on the offer. After we pried Fahima out of the rocker, the old couple gladly walked with David over to his house.

Emmett looked tired after a long day out with his friends, plus the shock of an intruder in his cottage. Without a word, he trundled off to bed.

The bongo drums were still thumping in my chest. There was no way I'd be able to sleep. I clipped a leash to Solow's collar, grabbed a flashlight and slipped out the front door. Moonlight reflected off the street, the leafy trees, lighting up the whole landscape. I didn't need the flashlight after all, at least not until we arrived at the foliage surrounding Emmett's cottage where everything was dark and hidden from the moon.

Solow pulled me forward, sniffing furiously. Finally, he stopped at the open cottage door, raised his head and howled, as if to say, "Someone has been messing around in my friend's cottage."

Shivering, even though it wasn't cold out, I flipped a switch and there was light. But light was not a comfort. Emmett's cot was on the wrong side of the room, slashed and ripped to pieces. I bent down and started sifting through the clutter on the floor.

Wham! I was hit from behind, lost my balance and fell flat onto painful bits of broken furniture. I quickly scrambled around and up onto my knees, coming face-to-face with a little goat named Lilly who licked my face. I quickly dropped the idea that Lilly had caused the catastrophe because the cot had been cut, not chewed. Even the naughtiest of goats could not have created this level of destruction.

Solow and Lilly did a little hello, how-are-you dance outside while I gathered my wits and picked myself up. I stepped outside to see how the kids were getting along.

A car door slammed.

Blood drained from my head down to my feet making them feel planted to the concrete walkway. The kid paid no attention to my commands. I grabbed Solow's leash and yanked him through the tall hedge and up the hill toward a row of spooky-looking eucalyptus trees bathed in moonlight. Lilly galloped in circles, bringing up the rear.

After a hundred yards of scrambling through high grass and shrubs, we reached the top of the ridge and headed down the other side. I collapsed on the ground, not even thinking about snakes, bugs or creatures that typically come out at night like bats, skunks and the occasional mountain lion.

Solow and Lilly butted each other in the grass as I strained to hear what was going on at the cottage. The bongos made it difficult to hear anything—in fact, I couldn't hear a thing except Solow and Lilly knocking their heads together. Between fear and curiosity, curiosity finally won. I crept a few yards up to the top of the ridge and looked down. Dim yellow light rose from the cottage skylights, lighting the air above the foliage. Obviously I'd forgotten to turn off the light.

As I watched, the light went off.

I shuddered. Someone had been in the cottage. As the kids frolicked, I strained to hear every sound, every cricket, every rustle of moving grass. Minutes went by like hours. The kids were restless. Finally, I heard a door slam, a motor start and headlights disappear into the night. After a few more minutes of listening, I cautiously made my way down to the road, and then sprinted over to my house.

I dropped Lilly off at the shed where she pigged out on alfalfa pellets and a bowl of sour apples before bed.

Solow and I quietly entered the house and went straight to our beds.

It was midnight and I couldn't sleep. I had way too much on my mind. I crept out of the bedroom wearing sweats and a t-shirt, leaving Solow to his dreams of chasing Fluffy. I tiptoed through the house and out the back door.

Bathed in moonlight, I waded through acres of tall grass growing between my house and David's. I crossed his patio and tapped on the sliding glass door. He immediately opened the door. Obviously he wasn't sleeping either.

"Josephine, what are you doing out this time of night?" he whispered.

"Feeling restless, I guess."

"Yeah, I know what you mean. I was feeling restless myself, a little curious too so I drove up to Emmett's property and took a look around. I hate to tell you, but the cottage is a smashed up mess."

Then it hit me. While I was running for my life and hiding in the grass, Solow didn't bark because he knew it was David. I took a deep breath, listened to the gentle snores coming from Rusty and Fahima's room down the hall, and leaned into David's embrace.

Luckily, David's room was dark and he couldn't see the foolish blush on my face. I decided to let it all go, to not think about the monster who'd cut the cot to ribbons. Instead, I decided to live in the moment and love in the moment and it was a good choice.

CHAPTER FIFTEEN

Thursday morning, I quietly opened the back door of my house and tippy toed down the hall.

Emmett suddenly opened the bathroom door and stepped out.

"Josephine, good morning. I'll start the coffee," he said, staring at my hair.

"That would be wonderful, Emmett. Did you sleep...?"

"...well? Not really. I dreamt someone was in and out of the house, back and forth all night. I guess I'm overly worried about my cottage. But there's nothing left to steal—nothing to worry about, is there?"

"I don't blame you for worrying, Hooley. I'm worried too."

Emmett turned and walked to the kitchen, shoulders sagging.

I continued down the hall to my room where Solow opened his droopy eyes and groaned. I collected up some clean paint-spattered clothes and headed back to the bathroom for a quick shower that turned into a long shower because I discovered that bits of grass and twigs were tangled in my hair. I finally joined Emmett at the kitchen table for coffee and toast prepared by my live-in gentleman friend, wearing sweats, an over-sized red and gold forty-niner shirt and flip flops. When I asked about his choice of footwear, he said he wanted to practice until the shoes submitted to his will.

I laughed and grabbed the closest section of newspaper and glanced at the articles, looking for something interesting to read but not expecting to find anything. I stopped searching when I saw a picture of the Prince and his painting on page three.

"Emmett, you missed the best, or maybe I should say, the most ridiculous part of the auction. The Prince bid on a...."

"...painting," Emmett said. "Yes, I saw the story in the paper yesterday. I couldn't take my eyes off of the painting. I feel like I've seen it before."

"If you come to the gallery with me some day you'll see a lot more like that one, and some nice paintings too. What are you planning for today, Emmett?"

"I thought I'd work on clocks."

"I was thinking we should pay Rose a visit at the old folks home. Did you say she was in Capitola?"

"Yes, yes, Capitola. I'd very much like to go for a visit."

"Okay, be ready to go when I get home this afternoon. I'll try to get off early." I grabbed my purse and the last piece of toast and headed out the door. Solow begged to go with me. I apologized for leaving him behind, tossed him my toast and drove off in a cloud of gravel dust. The morning fog had already cleared and the day was warming up nicely.

Alicia greeted me from near the top of the eight-foot ladder.

Athenian figures fighting Amazons were slowly coming alive thanks to strategically placed shadows and highlights. Fortunately for us, much of the mythical battle had been erased over the years, making our job simpler. The mural would be a scaled-down, close to fifty percent smaller, depiction of the west end of the Greek Parthenon.

I worked on a simulation of a design frieze and characters running across the building, ten feet up, just below the larger figures painted under the eves.

After half an hour of hard work, Kyle arrived. He offered to take Alicia's place on the ladder and she accepted. All morning and afternoon, we rotated our stations. I spent several sessions near the top of the eight-foot ladder and a few on the six-foot ladder just like my friends. By sharing the painting of each subject, our styles comingled into one style.

More paintings and two sculptures were delivered to the gallery, keeping Irene and Nico busy. Around three o'clock, wet fog blew into town, turning the place into a cold gray landscape. I used the chilly weather as my excuse for us to leave early, and my friends loved the idea. We cleaned up the paint, put everything away in the shed and drove home.

My home sat under blue sky going gray.

Emmett was anything but gray in his new slacks and Hawaiian shirt.

By the time I changed my clothes and we climbed into my truck, fog had engulfed the whole area. The wet stuff lasted all the way to Capitola.

Emmett showed me where to turn and where to park. The one-story building was modest and uncomplicated, built for maximum capacity back in the eighties.

"Emmett, do you think Rose will remember you?"

"Oh sure, she's coherent. It's Ed who thinks she's losing her mind," he grumbled. Emmett led the way to the main desk where we asked permission to see Rose. The receptionist told us to have a seat and wait to be escorted to Room Number 198. We sat in chairs at the far end of a large, well-populated room, listening to the muffled voices of disgruntled old people sitting in wheelchairs with glazed eyes and slack jaws.

A large, silver-haired woman wheeled herself across the room and parked in front of Emmett. Her beautiful face was wrinkle-free and her hands showed no signs of age.

"Rose, how are you dear?" he said as he stood, bent down and placed a kiss on the woman's rosy cheek. Her blue eyes sparkled.

"Oh, Emmett, I'm so happy to see you. I'm stuck here with all these drooling fools and I haven't had a real visitor in a long time. You look wonderful. I don't remember your dark hair and mustache, but then Ed says I don't remember much these days," she sighed.

"You can't remember my mustache because it's new," he chuckled. "Rose, may I present Ms. Josephine Stuart, a new friend of mine."

"Josephine...you're very young and pretty," she said, eyeing us back and forth.

"I'm happy to meet you, Rose. Emmett has told me all about you."

"Then you know that I'm working hard to get out of this place." Rose looked around the room to see who was listening. That was when I noticed the woman was strapped into her wheelchair.

"Did Ed tell you about Hilda?" Emmett asked.

"Yes, dear, I'm so sorry. Hilda was a lovely person and I considered her to be my best friend." Rose pulled a tissue from the pocket of her faded pink robe. "I thought you were in Arizona. Did you go to the convention this year...and the auction?"

"Yes, I did and Josephine went with me. We had a grand time," he smiled.

"Rose, are you able to walk...?" I asked, searching her person for a reason to be in the wheelchair.

"Rose can walk," Emmett said, "but Ed claims she falls easily."

Hoping to get away from the chair situation and Rose's angry look, I asked if her stepson was a regular visitor. She said she was glad he wasn't and dropped the subject. I noticed a folded quilter's magazine stuffed in a pocket attached to the side of the chair. In a desperate attempt to find a safe topic, I asked if she was a quilter.

Yes, Rose was a quilter, a proud winner of blue ribbons at the county fair twelve years in a row. She described some of her favorite creations in great detail and went on to say that sadly the quilts had all been sold. She wasn't able to keep even one for her own bed because Ed needed money. Actually, she no longer had her bed or her house. In fact, Ed had sold everything and moved into a one bedroom apartment in Santa Cruz.

Water welled up, half drowning her deep blue eyes, but Rose didn't let go of a single tear until it was time for us to leave. We stood up to go and the flood began.

Emmett leaned over, kissed Rose's wet cheek and hurried out the door.

I handed her my business card and told her to call if she needed anything. Rose patted my hand, smiling through her tears.

The damp air smelled fresh and sweet. I suddenly felt thankful for my freedom to move around in the world, and I felt profoundly sad for Rose. I caught up to Emmett.

"Poor Rose, I wish we could break her out of that place," I said.

"Yes, I know what you mean," he shivered as he slowly climbed into my truck.

Just as I opened the door on my side, I heard a loud crash and whipped my head around. Someone had just crashed through the glass entrance doors. I saw a wheelchair on its side, wheels spinning, its occupant bloody and struggling to free herself of the restraints.

Three nurses rushed through the frame of the door and circled the wheelchair. I heard someone crying. My heart was breaking. I knew who was in the chair and so did Emmett.

Should we go or should we stay? Emmett's face was pale and twisted, his breath short and shallow. Mine wasn't any better. We watched as Rose was loaded onto a gurney and taken inside.

Emmett made a little motion with his hand for me to go ahead and drive home.

Two silent torturous miles later, I whipped the truck around and drove back to the convalescent hospital and parked in a blue zone.

Emmett quickly climbed out of his seat, put a little speed to his gait and stepped through the shattered door.

I was right behind him, ignoring polite requests from a flustered receptionist. Rose had already been hauled away and we needed to find her. She and I had become fast friends and Emmett's wrinkles had turned into serious worry-lines.

The receptionist motioned for us to have a seat and wait. Emmett ignored her and kept walking, straight to Room 198 with me at his heels. The door was closed, barely muffling the shouting and crying inside. A man's voice boomed over all the other commotion.

"You do this one more time and you'll be living at the county hospital."

A man dressed in blue scrubs charged through the door, slammed it behind him and marched down the hall in an obvious huff.

Emmett and I looked at each other and headed for the front entrance. Apparently Rose had a history of escape and we didn't have the power to help her. Her injuries were probably minor since her indignant shouting was full-throttle.

The man in scrubs stopped at the front desk. I asked him about Rose.

"She needs an attitude adjustment," he said and walked away before I had time to give a good comeback.

The ride home felt long and way too quiet. What could I say to poor Emmett?

Solow greeted us with a soulful howl, as if he knew how we were feeling. I fed him his kibble and then began making dinner. I threw a meatloaf together, tossed it in the oven with a few potatoes and then flopped into a chair with the newspaper.

"Josephine, do you think Rose will be all right...you know...her injuries?" Emmett asked as he walked into the room.

"Don't worry, Hooley, the doctors and nurses will fix her up and she'll be fine. We need to see her again soon. I'll try to get away early again tomorrow and we'll go for a visit. She must be feeling desperate to be crashing through doors like that."

Hooley slouched into a chair next to me and held a section of newspaper at eye level. His hands shook and the paper rattled as he tried to collect himself.

I wasn't doing any better with my newspaper, reading the same sentence over and over. I finally put the paper down and checked the phone to see if I had any messages. Mom had called wanting to know if she could borrow my bowling ball. She and Dad were going to teach Myrtle how to bowl. The second call was from Dee. She gave a phone number, but no other message. I dialed the number. Dee answered.

"Josephine, thank you for calling. I just wanted to let you know that I didn't go to Peru with the Prince."

"What happened, Dee?"

"For one thing, the diamond necklace was for his mother. I should have known. But worse than that, his secretary—and you should see the big hussy—was also invited to go to Peru. This gal was all over him."

"I'm sorry it didn't work out, Dee. Where are you now?"

"I stayed the night with my mom in Gilroy and I thought I'd look you up today since I'm in the area."

I gave Dee directions to my house, put the baked potatoes and meatloaf on hold and chopped greens for a salad.

Emmett went outside to feed Lilly with Solow at his heels.

Minutes later, I heard a car crunch up the driveway and a door slam.

The old man escorted Dee into the house. She looked somewhere between a beautifully tanned desert-rat and a privileged jet-setter with a dusty backpack slung over one shoulder. Her turquoise necklace graced a designer jeans and silk blouse outfit.

After dinner, Dee and I sat at the table for over an hour talking about everything under the sun while Emmett cleared the table and then shuffled off to the living room.

"Dee, how did you meet the Prince? Was it on the hike to mount Kilimanjaro?"

"Actually, I met him at the base of the mountain. My party was scheduled to start the climb on a Tuesday, but some bad winds were happening so we waited another day and climbed on Wednesday with the Prince's party. The Prince and I talked about world affairs all the way to the top of the mountain and about love on the way down."

"Did you see him again?"

"Oh yeah, he took me to an art auction in LA. That's where we met Roy."

"Our local artist, Roy Miller?"

"Yep. That's when the Prince acquired his first Roy painting. I met Mr. Polyester and wasn't impressed, but he must be smarter than he looks. He talked the bodyguards into letting him give a painting to the Prince and then left the door open for the press. Several newspaper photographers crowded into the room and they were all snapping pictures. The front page was good advertising for Roy, and he instantly became a big-time player. Did you see what his last painting went for?"

"Yeah, I wouldn't have paid two bottle caps for that painting." I wrinkled my nose for effect. We played a couple games of scrabble and ended the evening with ice cream. I offered Dee the couch for the night. She accepted without hesitation.

I put my lap-top on the kitchen table, checked my emails and made some mental notes to myself like, call Mom and buy more ice cream. I finally shuffled off to the bedroom and discovered that Solow was not in his bed. Thinking that was very strange, I peeked into the living room. There was Dee, asleep on the rug with my "welcome-wagon" dog nestled against her lanky frame.

I crawled into my bed and punched in David's number. We talked and yawned for a few minutes and then said goodnight. Sweet dreams followed. But the last dream turned into a nightmare starring Rose. I watched her shimmy up a very tall flagpole, her robe blowing in the wind like a pink flag. She threatened to jump into a rocky koi pond below. The fish were flapping their fins, screaming hysterically and throwing themselves out of the water onto the pavement. They all escaped in little wheelchairs.

CHAPTER SIXTEEN

Early Friday morning my radio alarm blasted a rousing rendition of "Thriller."

I smacked the off-button, rolled over and crawled out of bed, noticing Solow was not in his bed. I slipped into my robe and walked to the kitchen where Dee and Emmett were discussing the stock market over coffee. I poured a cup for myself and sat with them at the table. I asked Dee if she had any plans for the day. She said she was free so I asked if she'd like to spend the day in Moss Landing. She thought it was a wonderful idea.

After a shower and light breakfast, I drove my truck to Moss Landing with Dee following in her rented silver BMW. We parked in front of the faux Parthenon. I introduced Dee to my friends and she immediately began helping us. She carried equipment from the shed and pumped us up with her compliments on the mural.

Kyle could not take his eyes off Dee. His pale complexion had turned rosy and then scarlet when he tripped on a wrinkle in one of the tarps.

When Irene and Nico arrived, they were happy to see Dee again. She followed them into the gallery but didn't stay long. When she came out, she said she enjoyed seeing the statues and glass sculptures, but Roy's paintings reminded her of the Prince.

For as long as I could remember, the unanswered question was: why do some people, the Prince included, pay good money for bad artwork? I felt like shouting, "The Emperor has no clothes, and Roy's paintings stink." But the haughty art world was like that. Whatever the fad was, follow it, frame it and one day forget it as the next new fad arrives on the scene. Who better than an actual Prince to accidentally promote a new artist and his style of work?

I volunteered for the eight-foot ladder while my caffeinated body still had enough energy, and went straight to work on the faux relief in the upper right corner of the mural, a chariot and three muscled men wearing loincloths.

Dee stood next to Alicia's ladder chatting away the morning. Luckily, Alicia was the type of painter who could balance on a ladder, paint random cracks on the pillars with precision, keep a conversation going and chew gum all at the same time.

After lunch, Dee said she wanted to explore Moss Landing and would see me later at the house. When I arrived at the house around five, no one was home but Solow. I helped my four-legged buddy into the passenger seat, fired up the truck and two minutes later parked in front of Emmett's ash heap. Solow and I made our way up to the cottage, checked inside and all around. No Emmett.

I pulled mail from the mail box, drove home and placed the envelopes on the steps leading up to the loft. Dee's backpack sat near the steps. The house seemed extra quiet and empty. Obviously Emmett and Dee had gone somewhere and were probably perfectly safe.

After jumping into clean clothes and making a few make-up and hair adjustments, Solow and I crossed the back field and entered David's house from the patio. He and Emmett finally looked up from the ball game on TV.

"Josie, how was work?" David asked.

"We got quite a bit done today—that is, Alicia and I got a lot done. Kyle was another story. He has a hard time painting with one eye on the wall and one eye on Dee. He can't even walk without tripping over his own feet," I laughed. "Where's Dee?"

"We thought she was with you," David said.

"She left us at noon. I'm sure she'll be back. Her backpack is still next to the steps. Speaking of steps...I picked up your mail today, Emmett. I left it on the steps to the loft."

"Thank you, Josephine. Was Lilly around?"

"I didn't see her," I said as I sat down next to David on the sofa and then scooted closer. He put his arm around my shoulder, his eyes fixed on the game. Sometimes our "romantic friendship" felt more like "old married couple."

"Josephine, do you think we might visit Rose this evening?" Emmett asked.

"Sure. David, why don't you come with us? The poor woman has a burr in her saddle. Maybe you can help us find a way to help her."

"Yeah, sounds good...after the game." David walked us to the back door and said he'd pick us up at seven-thirty.

Emmett and I trudged across the grassy field while Solow sniffed everything in sight and finally caught up to us at the house. I looked around. No BMW in the driveway and no sign that Dee had returned to the house.

After a simple dinner of left-over's, I called Dee's number. She didn't answer her cell phone so I left a message telling her where we were going, let her know that the back door would be unlocked and to make herself at home. I also left a note on the kitchen table explaining that we'd be visiting Rose Hymiller in case she didn't check her phone messages.

David picked us up at seven-thirty. His hair was a little damp and he smelled like old-fashioned soap, my favorite scent.

Emmett and Solow climbed into the back seat, the old Jeep engine turned over and we motored through Aromas, Watsonville and Aptos. By the time we entered the little seaside village of Capitola, the sun was sinking into the Pacific and smears of orange and red streaked the purple sky. Nature's lavish display of beauty stood in stark contrast with the institutional environment of the rest home.

I approached the desk and told the nurse that we wanted to see Rose.

The nurse pointed to a large woman wearing a faded pink robe and a big white bandage on her forehead.

Rose saw us and waved from her wheelchair parked in the far corner of the room.

Emmett had already spotted Rose and was working his way through a gauntlet of wheelchairs and sad-faced seasoned citizens. He bent down and kissed her cheek.

David and I were half-way across the room when an old-timer cut in front of me and parked his chair at my knees. He wanted to know my name and what year it was. A hefty nurse arrived, told the gentleman it was bedtime and wheeled him away.

By the time we arrived, Emmett had already settled into a chair beside Rose, who looked like she'd been in a war-zone. Besides the taped forehead, she had gauze and tape covering her left hand and left ear.

"Rose, I'd like you to meet my friend, David."

They shook hands.

I stepped behind the wheelchair so that David could chat with Rose. He inquired about her injured left hand.

I glanced at the familiar, dog-eared quilting magazine in her wheelchair pouch. It shared space with a packet of Kleenex and something turquoise at the bottom of the gaping pocket. I straightened the collar on her robe and massaged her shoulders as Rose described in detail all her injuries to David, who listened politely.

After thirty minutes of whining, she made her case for release and then came the tears. We were all sniffling by the time she came to her hapless future with no place to go—no place to live, ever.

"Hilda would have taken me in," she sobbed.

"I'm sorry, Rose," Emmett cleared his throat. "I no longer have a house." He reached for her hand, but she pulled it away. "Have you been in contact with Ed?"

"Are you kidding? He put me in this dirty bone yard…he won't even take my calls."

"I'll see if Roy can help…."

"Emmett, don't you call Roy! I'll find a way out of here on my own." Her jaw was set.

David brought Rose a cup of water. She took a couple sips, her hand relaxed and water splashed onto the floor. I picked up the paper cup and found a nurse to wipe up the water.

After an uncomfortable silence, we said our goodbyes and Rose wept as she rolled her wheelchair toward the door. A male nurse held onto the chair while we made our exit.

I turned and looked back through the glass. The tears were already gone.

We were quiet all the way home, except for Solow's snoring. My thoughts covered a multitude of conflicting ideas like was Rose depressed or demented, sad or cynical, lonely or lying, melancholy or manipulating? Was I crazy or confused for having such thoughts?

David dropped us off at my house, gave me a quick kiss and drove home.

My pickup stood alone under the Milky Way and a rising half-moon. Where was the BMW? Why hadn't Dee answered my phone call?

We entered the house. I flipped on a light. Dee's backpack sat next to the stairs, right where she left it. I told myself not to worry about the woman. After all, she'd slept on the floor of a cave, miles from civilization for almost a year. She'd hiked to the top of killer mountains and cavorted with a real Prince. So why was I worried? Maybe because, if I'd had a daughter, she would be around Dee's age.

Emmett gathered his mail and said he was going to bed.

The house phone rang.

I jumped, and answered the call on the second ring. The voice on the other end sounded strange, like a crank call. I was ready to hang up but then I heard my name and finally realized it was Dee calling. She sounded groggy, not her usual self-assured voice, as she explained that she would need a ride Saturday morning at eleven from Dominican Hospital in Santa Cruz. I asked her what happened.

"I was thinking about the Prince," she muttered. "I had Roy Miller's card in my purse...his paintings remind me of the good times we...the Prince and I...anyway, I decided to go see Roy's studio. I'll tell you all about it when I see you, if I can remember. I left his place and I remember stopping at a stop sign and then, wham! A bakery truck clipped the right back-side, and spun me around into on-coming traffic.

I think someone else hit the car after that. A nurse told me that paramedics had put me in an ambulance and drove me to Dominican Hospital."

"Don't worry about a thing, Dee. I'll pick you up at eleven."

She hung up without saying goodbye. That was when my maternal instincts shot into over-drive. How could Dee travel the world with confidence and then get slammed in the little ocean village of Capitola? Something smelled fishy.

CHAPTER SEVENTEEN

My eyes popped wide open Saturday morning at dawn. Remembering Rose's strange behavior and then my phone conversation with Dee Friday night made me uneasy all over again. For practical purposes, I put Rose out of my mind and concentrated on Dee's situation.

By seven a.m. I was dressed in non-paint clothes, backing my pickup down the driveway. I'd already found Roy Miller's address in the phone book, left a note for Emmett on the kitchen table and poured kibble into Solow's bowl. I squinted at the rising sun until the road finally headed west, leaving the sun behind me.

Half an hour later, I entered Capitola, turned into a narrow, dead-end alley, parked and walked one block to Number 92B. The old two-story stucco building faced a train trestle stretching across Soquel Creek, just one block from the ocean, probably the most picturesque spot on earth. A bike path ran along the levy between the river and a string of small apartment buildings built in the twenties and thirties.

Capitola was comatose. I didn't blame the village people. It was Saturday morning—time to sleep off Friday night. What was I thinking? Maybe that was the problem. I wasn't used to thinking before eight o'clock in the morning, before my usual two cups of coffee.

Emmett would be up by now, and David would probably drop by my house later.

After giving myself strong orders to focus on Roy, I climbed the stairs, stepped up to the weathered door labeled, "92B" and knocked. The knock heard round the town, or so it seemed, echoed off the high bank across the creek. Ducks and other water foul skittered up the river, some breaking into flight.

I knocked again and peeked through the closest window. If Roy was home, he had to be in the bathroom because his cluttered apartment was a one-room studio and he was nowhere in sight. His canvases and paints monopolized one end of the room. Cardboard boxes, a bed, a small TV and a tiny kitchen filled the rest of the space. I stared at the bathroom door for several minutes, and then let my eyes wander over to an unfinished canvas coated in familiar-looking smears of paint.

I finally gave up and walked back to my truck. It was almost eight-thirty. I had two hours to kill before I had to drive to the hospital and pick up Dee. I called Emmett.

"What are you doing in Capitola, Josephine?"

"Like I said, I'm checking on something Dee told me about. I'll pick her up at eleven."

"You'll tell me all about it when you come home?"

"OK, Hooley, gotta go." We hung up. If I wasn't comfortable telling Emmett about my hunch that something went wrong at Roy's house, I figured it would be worse with David. He was always quick to ask for help from the police. My methods were different. I wanted to know if a crime had actually been committed first. Police were the last resort.

I turned the key. The engine responded. I cranked the wheel to the right and backed into someone's short driveway. Just as I was about to roll forward and turn left toward Capitola Road, a white van passed in front of me and parked in the space I had vacated. I recognized Kat in the passenger seat. The driver fit Dee's description of Roy. He was pale and bone skinny with wild, curly black hair. His expression looked angry as he focused on Kat. The delivery gal didn't look happy either, but when did she ever look happy?

I watched the couple walk to Roy's apartment building, climb the stairs and disappear inside. I looked around for a parking space, thinking I might be able to talk to Roy after all. I finally squeezed into a parking space big enough for a smart car on Capitola Road, dropped two quarters in the meter and walked three blocks to Roy's place. I charged up the stairs just as the screen door swung open, smacking me in the nose.

Kat stood in front of me, her sausage arms wrapped around a large taped box.

"What do you want?" she snapped. "Aren't you one of the mural painters?"

"Yes, I'm Josephine," I said, automatically rubbing my insulted nose. "I need to talk to Roy."

"Why?"

"Because I owe him some money," I said as sweetly as possible.

Kat rolled her eyes, brushed by me and clomped down the stairs.

Roy came to the door carrying three canvases and a tool box.

Roy set the metal box on the floor by my foot. "Did you say you owe me some money? Or are you here to collect money?" he growled, picking up the tool box and pushing his way past me.

"I need to talk to you about Dee."

He stopped halfway down the stairs. "What about her? We didn't do nothin'."

"All I know is…" I gulped some air, "…my friend is in the hospital with a concussion. She said she came here to talk to you and that it didn't go well. What does that mean? How did it go? Was she nervous, ill, upset?" I wondered if I should show him how worried I was, or try to play it like a mother grizzly? Dee had mentioned something about Emmett's sister but I couldn't remember what she said while I was in the presence of "Roy, the Intimidator."

"Snotty rich girls don't impress me. I was minding my own business when she comes up here expecting to see some fancy work studio. I offer her a beer and a little fun. She says my place stinks. This is where I work, but not any more. I'm moving out…as you can see."

"Where are you moving?"

Roy threw his head back and laughed as he descended the last five steps and turned left, down the street, passing Kat who was empty-handed and headed in my direction.

I had no wish to be anywhere near Cranky Kat so I thundered down the stairs and took a right onto the riverfront bike path. I followed it into town, circled four bocks back to my pickup, dropped the last of my quarters into the meter, crossed the main street and entered the Mom & Pop Diner stuffed with tourists and locals having breakfast. The smell of coffee and maple syrup and the hum of a dozen different conversations calmed my nerves. I claimed the last empty seat, a stool at the counter, and sat down.

Without saying a word, a middle-aged waitress slopped the counter with a wet rag and then pushed a mug of hot coffee in front of me. I looked around to see what the most popular breakfast foods were.

Almost everyone had a stack of pancakes. Mine arrived shortly. I chose the "fancy cakes," chocolate chips on the inside and toasted pecans on the outside, topped with whipped cream, enough calories to keep an Olympic swim team fired up for days.

Halfway through the caloric pile I paused, hoping to make room for a couple more bites.

The room lost its chatty racket as people finished their breakfasts and waddled out the door like over-fed penguins dressed in colorful summer wear. I paid my bill and headed for the front door. My pancakes lurched when I saw blue, black and red splashes of paint smeared across a large canvas hanging near the door. Hand printed in black ink, the price tag said two-hundred dollars. Two blue-ink zeros had been added making the price twenty-thousand dollars, a bargain compared to the Arizona auction price.

The gal who'd waited on me looked up as she scrubbed a table top.

"Like it?"

I rolled my eyes.

"At least one person likes it," she laughed.

"How do you know that?"

"He brings her in every Tuesday night. She's way older, might be his mother. Anyway, she can't stop talking about how famous he is. You'd think he won the dang Peace Prize or something."

"Who pays for the meal?"

"He does, now that he's rich," she laughed.

"So the woman-friend used to buy Roy's dinner before he got rich?"

She nodded, and headed back to the counter.

"Wait a minute, I wanted to ask if you saw the accident yesterday. You know, the bread truck and the BMW."

The woman said she heard the crash a block away, but didn't see the vehicles involved. The restaurant had been busy at the time. She remembered glancing out the window as the ambulance screamed into town.

I thanked her and left the building, wishing I'd learned more about Dee's visit to Capitola. I crossed the street, walked two blocks to the esplanade, sat down on a concrete bench and watched endless rows of sea-green water rise, curl, crash and dissipate into the wet, bubbling sand. My senses were stimulated by the scent of decaying seaweed, the shrieking of gulls and the glint of brilliant sunshine on the water. It was a beautiful play without a plot and I was in a trance.

The trance ended when a mom, pushing a stroller full of screaming twins, rolled by.

Questions popped into my head. Roy was obviously moving. What if he'd done something awful to Dee and I never had another chance to find him? Suddenly I remembered what Dee had said— something about Roy not being Roy.

I still had forty-five minutes before I needed to get back on the road to pick up Dee at the hospital. I stood up and stretched. It was a perfect day for a walk along the esplanade which connected to the bike path fronting Roy's place. In less than ten minutes I was standing at his door. I peeked in the window. All the boxes were gone. A naked bed, a couple chairs, one lamp and one little rusty table were all that was left, if you didn't count the clutter on the floor and a couple large painted canvases leaning against the far wall.

I tried the doorknob. It turned. I stepped inside. To me, the canvases were part of the litter, but I was pretty sure Roy wouldn't leave them behind. I heard footsteps and whirled around.

Roy suddenly appeared in the doorway with a crafty smile on his pale face.

"Is this what you do for a living—break into people's homes?"

"Sorry, I thought you'd moved out." Heat crept up to my cheeks. "I came here hoping to talk to you...."

"I bet. Maybe you know how much these canvases are worth. How do I know you weren't trying to steal them?"

I held myself back from a good eye-roll and I did not point a finger down my throat. Instead I made up some bilge about the existential value of priceless psychotic imagery on canvas. I told him he'd captured the essence of neurotically suppressed ambivalence in every stroke. His chest puffed out when I told him that magnificent affluent pauperism was plain to see in all his works of art.

Roy's sarcastic smile turned into a catfish-grin. The catfish had a wiggly worm in his mouth, but hadn't figured out that it was rubber, made in China.

While I had him on the hook, I asked him a few questions. "Roy, do you remember how Dee looked yesterday? Did she look ill? Was she nervous about something?" My heart pounded in my chest as I looked up into flaring nostrils.

Roy moved closer and looked down.

His breath was hot and sour on my face.

"She looked snoopy—like you. She wanted to know things that are none of her business," he snarled, as the catfish hit the rubber.

I sidled toward the front door.

Roy followed and put a finger in my face. "Go back to Aromas. You're a pest."

I fled the apartment, fast-walked four blocks and took off in my truck, wondering how Roy knew where I lived.

I thought about Dee's visit with Roy. Did he mistreat her? Maybe Dee had made a driving error that caused the accident, or maybe the bread truck driver was drunk. All I could do was talk to Dee. I picked her up at the hospital and we talked all the way home. Unfortunately, she had only a partial memory of sipping a beer at Roy's, slipping on the steps and then the car accident. She showed me where she'd scraped her elbow but didn't remember why she fell down the stairs.

In the end, I let go of Dee's accident because I really needed to think about Emmett's problems. Dee was young. She could sort things out for herself. But Emmett was old, someone didn't like him and I was his designated protector. With all that in mind, I rechecked my mental list that Emmett had compiled of people who might do him harm.

Dee curled up on the couch and fell asleep while Emmett and I talked about a visit with Ed, who lived in Santa Cruz. Since my parents also lived in Santa Cruz, we'd deliver my bowling ball to them. Mom and Dad were a couple wrinkles short of eighty, but still enjoying life at a pretty fast pace. Dad had his bowling league at the Bowl and Bowl. Mom fussed over a couple rose bushes in the back yard, and belonged to the Rose Club where her personality really shone. She knew how to dress perfectly for all her clubs, activities and special occasions. Her pedigree, a special built-in sense of style that she was born with, had skipped my generation.

Dad was a master at searing sausages on the back yard barbeque, and Mom knew the basics at the kitchen stove—nothing exciting, but at her age that was enough. They were healthy, happy and inquisitive, and I couldn't wait to prove to them that the man living in my house really was almost ninety years old.

CHAPTER EIGHTEEN

Saturday afternoon Emmett agreed to go with me to see Ed, admitting that he was looking forward to getting out of the house but not excited about a visit with his nephew—Rose's husband and "jailer." He called Ed while I left a note for Dee and a rawhide bone for Solow.

Emmett repaired to the loft and changed into his Hawaiian shirt, khakis and flip flops.

When he came back to the kitchen, I stared at his feet, shaking my head warily.

"It's OK, Josephine. I've been practicing," he grinned. "They're starting to walk with me."

It was a great day to be out driving. But halfway through Aromas, I was sorry I hadn't secured my bowling ball a little better than just dropping it into a cardboard box. With wild abandon, the box and its occupant thundered back and forth across the truck bed as we drove out of the foothills.

A new green carpet of grass covered the earth, and the air was springtime warm and fresh. As we left the Aromas Hills behind, I happened to notice two cars and a white van in my rearview mirror. I stomped on the gas. We left the van behind as the bowling ball crashed into the tailgate.

After an enjoyable ride through half of Santa Cruz County, I'd forgotten all about the van until we arrived at Ed's little apartment in Santa Cruz. I looked around the parking area. The vehicle was nowhere in sight.

Ed's apartment complex consisted of several two-story wood buildings about thirty years old, smothered in a fresh coat of forest green paint with white trim and shaded by at least a dozen large redwood trees.

Emmett pointed up to Ed's little porch.

I grabbed a sweater from the cab and followed Emmett along a shady path and up a set of mossy stairs to Ed's second story apartment. A tree cast its dark shadow over Ed's little porch. Tiny mushrooms pushed through the cracks. I waited for the door to open, anticipating the monster Hooley had described.

The door finally opened.

"Hooley, old boy," Ed said as he looked us over. "Hardly recognize you with the haircut...mustache... and look at you, wearing flip flops. You look ten years younger. I wish Hilda could see you now." After an awkward silence, he ushered us inside.

Emmett introduced us.

Ed had wild curly hair and dark eyes like Emmett's, plus a double chin. He stood about six inches taller than Emmett and his handshake was hefty like his build. Looking around the modest front room, I decided he was a computer geek. Whatever he was working on took up all available surfaces, including the kitchen table.

"What are you working on?" I waved my hand around the room.

"I'm writing a book...the story of our family coming to America."

Emmett's jaw dropped, but he didn't say a word.

"Wow, that's quite an undertaking." Especially for the lazy, no good person Emmett had prepared me for.

I pressed Ed for a synopsis of the story, but he said he was a little disorganized at the moment and would we like a cup of coffee. Even before we said "yes" on the coffee, he was clearing away research books, notes and pieces of manuscript from the table. Coffee was served in three mismatched cups with apologies about a lack of cream and sugar.

Emmett ran a thumb up and down his coffee mug, eyebrows pressed together.

"Ed, where were you the evening of May fourth?"

"How should I know…oh, you mean the night your house caught on fire?"

"The night it was set on fire."

Ed opened his mouth, but decided not to speak. His jaw tightened, his eyes blazed.

I admired Hooley's direct approach but knew it wouldn't get us anywhere.

"Sorry, Ed, we're just trying to figure out who would have done such a thing, and we thought you might be able to help us." I squinty eye contacted with Emmett.

He relaxed his white knuckle grip on the mug.

"You think it wasn't an accident?" Ed cocked his head to one side. "I read in the *Sentinel* they think it was a homeowner accident."

Emmett's face turned red. Fortunately his words caught in his throat.

"The police are investigating," I said. "We have reason to believe it was a burglar who intentionally set the fire…explosion, really. Is there anyone in the family who'd do such a thing, maybe for revenge? Someone who's mentally ill? I'm worried about Emmett's safety."

"There was that fellow who stole change from the March of Dimes jar, and Hooley turned him in…remember that, Emmett…about three years ago?" Ed gazed at the ceiling as if to recall the facts.

Emmett cleared his throat. "That was Arnie. Hilda and I had lunch at the German Hall. Later, I happened to walk through the kitchen and found Arnie stuffing his pockets from the club safe. We never locked the safe during the day. We'd never needed to."

"Did he threaten you?" Ed asked.

"Not really, but the next week he was there when I parked my truck at the club house. Later, I went out to the truck to get my newspaper. I caught Arnie putting handfuls of dirt in my gas tank. He said he saw a kid doing it, but I saw Arnie doing it. It was my word against his, of course."

"Did Arnie know about your inheritance…the recipe?" Ed asked.

"The beer recipe you and everyone else wants?" Emmett glared at Ed. "His mother knew all about it, thanks to Hilda. My poor sister was not good at keeping secrets."

"Oh my gosh," I sputtered, "Arnie was right there in the room when you put your wooden box in the safety deposit box." I instantly covered my mouth with my hand. I looked at Ed to see if he knew about Hilda's tool box. He had a quizzical look on his face. Had I let the cat out of the box?

The conversation was heating up, but I couldn't wait any longer. I asked about the lady's room and Ed pointed down the hall. On the way back, I leaned into the one and only bedroom. A jumble of framed pictures adorned a walnut dresser-top. A group picture caught my attention because two of the figures were blacked out. I stepped closer and recognized the two worn-out hats I used to see traveling down Otis Road, riding in the eighty-four Chevy truck.

I walked into the kitchen, right in the middle of a discussion about Rose. Why was she living in the old folk's home? Why not? She was mentally ill and hard to handle. You couldn't handle Rose? I'd like to see you handle her. The poor woman is tied to a wheelchair…yada yada yada. They looked ready to punch each other.

I broke into the conversation that was going nowhere.

"Ed, Rose is very depressed…."

"Rose is out of control. You have no idea," he growled.

"How is your son Leroy doing? Does he visit Rose?"

"He's doing great. I don't know if he visits Rose and I don't care. All I know is, he's making money and I don't have to worry about him anymore." Ed's shoulders twitched. He stroked his damp forehead with one hand.

Emmett stood up and told Ed that my mother was expecting us and we had to leave. His flip flops barely kept up with his fast retreat to the truck.

We had a short visit with Mom and Dad and gladly handed off my bowling ball to be used by Myrtle. I figured the whole bowling thing was a ruse to get me over there so they could meet Mr. Hooley, and it had worked. Mom poured the tea and Emmett told a few cuckoo clock jokes. He seemed to enjoy my folks and Mom's peanut butter cookies.

Dad offered to take him bowling someday, a high honor in "Bob's World."

Mom asked us to stay for dinner but I explained that David had offered to take us to the wharf in Monterey for dinner. She fancied a wedding someday and would never stand between me and David. She shooed us out the door, telling me to drive carefully and watch out for the protesters on Pacific Avenue.

I tried circling around downtown Santa Cruz to avoid the protesters, but my usual route was closed. Two police cars were angled across the four lanes and a temporary sign pointed to River Street as an alternate route. I swerved onto River just as a large group of under-dressed protesters met up with half a dozen over-dressed policemen wearing helmets and riot gear.

Bam! Something exploded, sending a screen of smoke across my windshield.

Emmett ducked down in his seat, hands wrapped over his head.

"Hang on, Hooley. I'll get us out of here." I cranked the wheel hard. We did a U-ee and took off toward Mom and Dad's neighborhood.

When the air cleared, Emmett sat up straight and put his hands down. His head jerked back against the seat as he sucked in some air.

I pretended not to notice how distraught the poor man looked as we headed south to Mission Street and finally the freeway. We talked very little on the way home.

David met us at the door dressed like the handsome date he was.

"What's wrong with Emmett?" he whispered as the old man slumped into the sofa.

"He had to deal with his cousin and a bunch of protesters. I'll tell you about it later."

I asked Emmett if I could get him some tea or something to eat. He said he preferred to rest a while and later he'd snack on cold chicken. He wasn't acting depressed, just tired, so I finally gave up trying to get him to go with us to Monterey. Before we left the house, I warned him to lock the doors and not let anyone in.

My handsome date drove us into the setting sun and then headed south on Highway One to Monterey, asking questions the whole way. Like, was Ed as evil as Emmett thinks he is? Is he retired? Does he visit his wife at the old folks home?

I didn't have much to say about Emmett's cousin. It was too soon to know his real nature. I couldn't pin down a motive for Ed hurting Hilda and Emmett, but I kept him on my list of suspects.

Our Saturday night date started off with soft music and lots of talking and giggles. We were best friends who loved each other. Whether we were "in love" or not, I hadn't decided. We had been friends for over ten years, enjoying each other's company, ignoring our differences. David had a practical, measured, male way of looking at life. I tended to overreact and deal with life like a mother wolf with PMS defending her pups. David liked to let the authorities take care of problems. I preferred to "fix" everything myself, including Emmett.

"Josie, how's Emmett doing—any signs of depression?"

"I think he's OK. He tires easily. I would too if I was almost ninety."

"While you two were gone today, Lilly and I took a walk up to Emmett's place. I collected Emmett's mail and watered the fruit trees. I found this on the walkway behind his house, or what's left of the house. Anyway, it's a nail with a bit of plaster stuck to it." He kept one hand on the steering wheel, pulled the nail out of his pocket and held his hand out so I could see it.

"Emmett told me the house was made out of redwood on the outside. This nail must be from an inside wall, but how did it get outside?" I scratched my head.

"Something arrived in the mail for Emmett. The box had his name and your address. It was from the Sheriff's office." He cocked his head hoping to get an explanation from me. I thought about it.

"Was it heavy and smaller than a breadbox?"

"Yeah, it seemed heavy for its size."

"I wonder if it was Hilda." I turned to look at David's reaction.

He was silent for a minute and then his jaw dropped. "Are you saying it's her ashes?"

"Could be. Where did you put the box?"

"I left it on the counter by the back door. I wonder if he'll see it." David parked the jeep a block away from the wharf, the closest space available. "Think we should stay and have dinner?"

"Sure. We'll eat fast and go home. Emmett should be all right until we get back." That was not how I really felt. I pictured the old man opening the box, crying his eyes out and then searching the shed for a rope.

There was a twenty-minute wait for a table at our favorite restaurant so we hurried down the wharf to another fish place with less ambiance and fewer customers. It seemed like an eternity before we were seated. The waitress walked like her shoes weighed fifty pounds each. We gulped our food and left the bill and money near the register on our way out the door. The greeter woman asked if we enjoyed our dinner, but her words were lost as the door closed behind us.

It was an unusually clear night, a bit chilly, smelling of seaweed and clam chowder. Throngs of tourists sauntered up and down the length of the wharf while we tramped a zig-zag pattern around and through the crowds in an effort to get home quickly.

Occupying the passenger seat was difficult for me. I desperately wanted to push the gas peddle to the floor and pass every car on the highway.

David drove the speed limit and he drove me nuts—sitting there looking calm. But in the light of on-coming cars I noticed his tight jaw, shoulders leaning forward and worry lines pushing his eyebrows closer together. We had both seen what depression could do to poor Emmett.

Finally, the Jeep bumped up my driveway, stopping just short of the dark porch. We leaped out of the car and ran to the front door. It was locked.

"Emmett, open the door!" I shouted.

We listened for a minute. I pounded on the door again.

The door cracked open slowly and Emmett peeked out.

I drew in a breath. Tears stung my eyes.

"What is wrong, Josephine?"

"Nothing at all," I choked.

CHAPTER NINETEEN

Sunday morning came with sunshine and song birds, coffee and cinnamon rolls. Too bad Dee couldn't stick around long enough to enjoy it all. She took a call on her cell phone at seven-thirty a.m., thanked me for whatever, grabbed her backpack and raced out the door. The call had come from a woman in a black Lincoln sitting in my driveway. I thought the woman looked a lot like Dee but older. They left and I stepped away from the window.

I had no special Sunday plans. Emmett swept the patio while I dusted, vacuumed, mopped and scrubbed. I found him later, asleep in a contoured plastic chair on the patio with Solow at his feet.

I heard something, looked up and shaded my eyes.

David appeared like a dream from the grassy field.

Fluffy bounced along at his side.

Solow's eyes popped open. He took off after the contrary cat, and minutes later dragged himself home, his tail tucked between his legs. Fluffy jumped into David's arms and Solow looked the other way. Typically, the dog and cat had no problem sharing a small room with each other for many hours. It was the great outdoors that set them off.

David followed me into the house. He asked about Emmett. I told him the old man wanted to shop for an urn for Hilda's ashes, and I'd promised I'd take him shopping to find one.

"So where does one shop for an urn?" he asked.

"I'm thinking, antique store?"

David nodded thoughtfully, and then asked about Dee.

"She must be feeling all right. She left early this morning, backpack and all." No long goodbyes for that girl. I wondered if I'd hear from Dee in the future. For a while I had the feeling she was interested in helping Emmett solve the Hilda murder case. Apparently something better came up. I imagined her traveling across various continents with a Prince, a Baron—maybe a CEO or a president of something. Or maybe she went back to her cave in the desert. Either way, she was more adventurous than I.

"Hey, I just remembered an antique store we could take Emmett to, in Moss Landing."

"We, Kemosabe?"

"I just thought you might like…."

"…to be with you on your day off," he teased, wrapping an arm around my shoulders and planting a kiss on my forehead. "Anything new in finding a permanent home for Emmett?"

"I don't know that he's been looking, but he should. He can't live with me forever." My face prickled. For the first time, I heard myself expressing a wish for more private time with David. His quick smile doubled the heat in my cheeks.

An hour later, David, Emmett, Solow and I jammed into the Jeep and rode twenty miles to Moss Landing. By that time, we were all starving for lunch, and Bill's beckoned to us with the smell of French fries and deep-fried calamari. Emmett and David went inside to order while I stayed outside holding Solow's leash. He lurched forward toward a group of seagulls on the deck railing. I pulled him back. Solow pulled harder, ready for a good bird chase.

"Cool it, Solow! We didn't come here to chase birds."

Solow finally relaxed on the warm wooden planks and closed his eyes for an afternoon nap.

I watched a young family two tables away as they ate fish and chips. The youngest son obviously didn't like fish. His plate had barely been touched, except for the fries. When the family wasn't looking he walked his plate to the garbage can located near the railing full of birds. Their fiendish eyes followed him. He lifted the floppy paper plate up, aiming for the can, but the fish pieces fell on the deck before he let go of the plate.

Solow was suddenly awake and hurling his body forward, across the deck, obviously dazzled by deep-fried fish.

Jerked to my feet and flying behind my crazed dog, I hung onto the leash with both hands as we entered bird-territory.

The gulls came at us, ready to fight for every piece of spilt fish.

The little boy screamed and waved his arms over his head to keep the birds away.

Startled parents leaped toward the boy, and the father scooped him up into his arms.

Solow took his eyes off the fish for a second as he dodged the family. And then his brakes failed. He slid past the pieces of fish and the garbage can. His body didn't stop until his front half was under the railing, head down, hanging over foamy sea water that gently surged against a rock sea-wall.

I crouched down and grabbed Solow's hind leg. It was a good plan until a seagull dove at me, yanking a tuft of hair out of my head. I screamed and Solow's leg wiggled free. His body slipped further until his back feet left the deck. I quickly dropped the leash, not wanting to hang poor Solow by the neck. I watched in slow motion as he began his reluctant dive into the water.

After splash-down, I watched and waited for Solow's head to bob to the surface. I waited a few seconds more and then sprinted across the deck, hung a right at the stairs and another right onto the large rocks used to keep the ocean from eroding the land. After a short downward climb, I kicked off my flip flops and jumped into the cold frothy water.

I took a deep breath and submerged myself. Murky water stung my eyes as I searched for Solow. I saw movement and swam deeper toward a shadowy dog with his leash wrapped up in a submerged bicycle. There was no time to think about how a bicycle ends up in the drink, along with rusted steel bed springs and some other weird stuff. I went straight to my poor sweet dog and unhooked his leash. I desperately needed air and Solow didn't look good either. I quickly grabbed his collar and pushed off with my legs from the cluttered sandy bottom. We only had to travel about ten feet up, but Solow was no help at all. I popped up to the surface gasping, sucked in air and then started pulling Solow the short distance to shore. It was only a few yards but seemed like a mile.

I leaned against the rocks and lifted Solow's head and shoulders onto the shore. He didn't move. Salt water washed back and forth over his wet fur. I pushed him further up on the rocks until half his body was free of the surf, and then pulled myself out of the water—no easy task when fully clothed. I sucked in big gulps of air and let out a bucket of hot tears.

"Josephine…what happened…? I'll be right there." David yelled from the deck. Next thing I knew, he was beside me, pulling Solow up onto his lap. We talked to him, massaged his cold, wet body and prayed.

We heard a bark and turned to look under the deck. A sea lion, representing a large colony of lounging sea lions, swam closer and barked again.

Solow twitched.

"Solow heard the bark!" I cried, and then all the seals resting on heavy planks under the deck began to bark, and made a mass exodus into the water for a swim.

Solow opened his eyes.

David flicked a tear from his eye. "He's breathing, sweetie, and you're shivering." He stood up with Solow in his arms. I grabbed the backside of David's belt and let him pull me up and across the rocks to the sidewalk. By that time, Solow was looking around, eying the birds on the rail as if it was their fault he plunged into the ocean.

We met up with Emmett at a sunny table on the deck where he sat guarding our plates from the hungry sea gulls. He looked shocked when he saw us.

I found a comb in my purse and pulled it through my wet tangled hair while David ran to the Jeep for a blanket and an extra jacket. He swaddled Solow in the wool blanket and draped a down jacket over my shoulders. Solow and I shivered together until the sun finally warmed us.

We kept Solow wrapped in the blanket because we had no leash. Each of us shared some of our lunch with him to celebrate his return to life.

"Josie, do you feel up to shopping?" David asked.

"I'm Ok, but Solow needs a nap in the Jeep." So that's where we left him while we walked the town. Even though we rummaged through every antique shop, we were unable to locate a single urn.

We filed into the Jeep and David fired up the engine.

"David, look down the street. What's all that yellow tape for?"

Instead of heading toward the highway, he drove us to the tape at the end of the road, which happened to be in front of the Halikias Gallery.

One officer sat in the driver's seat of a parked patrol car.

I jumped out of the Jeep and approached the cruiser, forgetting how rumpled and scary I must have looked after my swim with the seals.

The window came down and a pair of icy-blue eyes met mine.

"Deputy Lund, what's going on?"

"A burglary." Her eyes glanced at my unruly hair and wrinkled clothes. She almost smiled.

"Can you tell me what was burgled?"

"No Ma'am. We're conducting an investigation." She turned back to her notebook, dismissing me like a fly on her cupcake.

While Officer Lund concentrated on writing her report, I stepped over to the front door which happened to be open a crack. I peeked inside.

"Ms. Stuart, can I help you?" Officer Sayer asked. "Stay there and don't touch anything."

"I work here...and I, ah was just wondering what was stolen." My eyes searched the walls as I spoke. Two of Bonni's beautiful watercolors were missing plus all of the useless monstrosities by Roy Miller. The place looked much better without his paintings.

"As far as we know, eight paintings were taken and the back door was damaged."

"When did it happen?"

"The owners of the gallery reported it this morning. We were called onto the case about an hour ago." He pointed a camera at the empty wall. "Sorry, you can't come in."

"Thank you, Officer." I headed back to the Jeep, wondering what kind of burglar would steal ugly paintings. I climbed into the passenger seat and David put the car in reverse.

"Your mural is looking good, honey. What did you find out from the deputy?" He turned the Jeep south, to the highway and then north to Watsonville.

"The thief has no taste in artwork...and Officer Sayer told me some of what happened. The back door looked like they used an electric saw...they massacred it. I wonder if an alarm went off. Eight paintings are missing. Six of them should have been burned a long time ago."

David gave me a funny look so I explained how ugly Roy's canvases were.

Emmett and Solow napped in the back seats and eventually my head dropped back and I closed my eyes. I dreamt I was under water trying to save my dog. Every time I tried to unhook Solow's leash, a wave would push me away. Over and over, I fought my way back to him. Just as I finally grabbed his collar and was about to reach the surface, something tugged at my shoulder. In my dream, it was a sea lion keeping me from surfacing and taking in the air I desperately needed. But when I woke up it was David.

"Hey Josie, wake up!" He kept his right hand on my shoulder, the left on the wheel.

"Huh? What happened?"

"Honey, you were making whimpering noises. Are you OK?"

"It was awful—a real nightmare," I shuddered.

We were half way to Watsonville when I decided it would be fun to stop in at Alicia's. David seemed OK with the idea and Emmett wasn't conscious yet. I needed a little time with my friend, some girl talk, and I knew David enjoyed talking sports with Ernie.

David parked the Jeep in front of the Quintana home. The boys in the back woke up and we all scrambled out of our seats. Halfway to the front door, we looked up at twenty sets of wings flapping overhead. A perfectly synchronized vee-shaped gaggle of Canadian geese had flown up from the lake behind the house, over the two-story roof-top and into the sun—honking in unison.

Trigger met us at the door, took Emmett by the arm and led us to the back yard where his parents were relaxing on lawn furniture. They looked surprised to see us—understandably.

"Hey guys, good to see you," Ernie said as he stood and shook hands with the men and a hug for me. "We were bird watching until they decided to fly away. Happens everyday at four o'clock. They have a great sense of timing."

Alicia asked if we wanted anything to drink.

"I would love a cup of hot tea," I said as we headed back to the house.

"Are you sure you don't want iced tea. It's such a nice day…."

"I know but once I get cold it takes me awhile to warm up."

I shivered and followed Alicia to the kitchen. She put the tea kettle on. A giant pot of beans simmered on the stove and a pie cooled on the sideboard. At first I was reluctant to talk about what happened at Bill's, unwilling to disturb the peace and harmony in Alicia's comfy kitchen.

"Jo, what happened to you? You look like you've been through a war or something."

"War with the birds," I laughed. "The good part of my story is that our mural is untouched. The worst is that we almost lost Solow. He almost drowned." I felt a knot in my throat as I began telling Alicia what had happened to Solow and then went on to tell about the burglary.

Shocked one minute, and laughing the next, she said, "That's the best thing that could have happened to the gallery. Roy's paintings were muy feo." She wrinkled her nose.

"Yeah, but was the gallery insured...and the watercolors are a real loss. I always liked Bonni's work." I looked up when Trigger ran into the room.

"Auntie Jo, did you know that I found Mama's sister, Eva, on the computer? She's on my Facebook right now. We saw pictures of her daughter, Dolores. She's my cousin," he grinned. "My cousin is a grown-up lady and she's been to Africa. I hope she takes me with her next time."

Alicia laughed. "It's true, Trigger found my family." She ruffled his hair. "I can't wait to see them face to face, but they're traveling right now and will call me when it's a good time for a visit. It's amazing how we only live about thirty miles from each other. They live in Gilroy. Eva works as an accountant at the Garlic factory. I think Dolores attends college somewhere."

I could not have been happier for my friend, until I asked about her oldest sister. Alicia said she was deceased, but didn't know the details yet. Eva would tell her what happened to the eldest sister and her mother when they met.

"Jo, did I tell you that Kyle's coming over for dinner tonight...actually in about a half hour. His girl friend broke up with him last week, and Friday he looked so sad. I told him I'd bake an apple pie if he would come here for dinner tonight. I hope you plan to stay and help me console our poor friend."

"Well, if you put it that way, I guess we have to," I grinned. I couldn't have been happier, especially since I hadn't planned anything for dinner and didn't feel like cooking. David and Emmett got the same invitation from Ernie and they responded enthusiastically.

CHAPTER TWENTY

Monday's working conditions at the gallery were impossible. Nico was impossible. He grumped around as if it was our fault his back door had been an easy entry. Detectives determined that an amateur thief had penetrated the Parthenon, and Nico wasn't happy. We tried ignoring him, but he paced the sidewalk as well as inside the building. Irene finally hauled him off to Bill's for an early lunch.

I had no desire to eat at Bill's again, at least not in this current century. Not with those beady-eyed birds begging for scraps. They cost Solow his dignity and nearly his life. Sunday, after almost drowning, he shivered every time he heard a noise and wouldn't leave my side. It wasn't until Monday morning that he finally regained his confidence.

Emmett had given Solow a good back scratch and some bites of his breakfast burrito.

I was just as bad. I plopped a scoop of ice cream on top of his kibble before I took off for work.

Work dragged on. We were eighty percent finished with the Parthenon and my mind had moved on to our next project, due to start in two weeks. For the next three or more days we'd continue to work on the intricate "sculpted relief" representation along the top of the building, plus faux "carved stone" details over and around the doorway. Alicia brought an eight-foot ladder from home so that two of us could work along the top and the third person would use the six-footer for the door area.

Nico wasn't the only grumbler. Kyle hadn't bothered to show up for dinner at Alicia's Sunday night and Monday wasn't much better. He arrived at the gallery an hour late, crabbed about having to work along the top of the building and insisted on going to lunch at Bill's for a cheese sandwich right after I suggested Dina's Deli further up the road.

Alicia and I rolled our eyes and went along with Kyle's plan.

We ordered lunch and found a table inside, even though Kyle said he wanted to be outside on the deck.

"So why does everyone want to be inside?" Kyle asked as we waited for our order.

"Because I hate those beady-eyed gulls and because of them, Solow fell off the deck yesterday and almost drowned."

"But he didn't drown…like, what's the big deal?"

"It was a big deal, but I guess you had to be there to understand." My mind went back to Solow as he struggled to escape his tangled leash. My face burned when I thought about the pile of junk at the bottom of the ocean. Someone had unloaded their bed springs, rusty bicycle and…."

"Jo, they called our number." Alicia pushed away from the table and led us to the pick-up area. We carried our entrees back to the table and half an hour later, I had to admit that Bill's was a good idea. Kyle picked up our empty plates and dumped them in the trash can. His mood had improved greatly.

My friends went back to work, but I was feeling restless. I rounded the Parthenon and slowly walked to the back door where Deputy Sayer sat on his haunches, making a plaster cast of someone's foot print in the wet sand. The wet sand happened to be about ten feet from the back door, near the rock seawall. Sayer looked up.

"Ms. Stuart, your mural is looking very real, like an old Greek building."

"Thanks. We call it the Parthenon. Painting is fun but I'd love to be doing what you're doing right now. Have you any ideas about who burgled the place?"

"Even if I did, I couldn't tell you. But if you have information, you can tell me," he grinned.

"By the way, how is the Hooley investigation coming along?"

The deputy cleared his throat and explained that there was only so much time in the day, bla, bla.

The minute Deputy Lund appeared on the scene, I headed back to my work. My young compadres worked from their eight-foot ladders. I climbed four rungs on the six-footer and began laying in shadows and highlights of an ancient Greek chariot pulled by thundering horses above the doorway. I imagined Charlton Heston driving the chariot.

Half an hour before quitting time, a black van parked next to my truck. Two men disappeared into the gallery. Minutes later they came back, each carrying a large box. The boxes were stowed in the van and the men went back for more. We were used to seeing items brought in, but not taken out. After several trips and many boxes, the van left.

Irene opened the door and looked out, not realizing that I stood on a ladder inches from the door way. I heard her sigh as she watched the van cross the bridge, heading for the highway.

"Irene, what's happening?" I said as I descended the ladder.

"Oh…nothing. Actually, the Chihuly glass is gone. They don't want to risk…."

"I'm sorry, Irene. I really don't understand this whole burglary thing. I never liked Roy's paintings and I can't imagine anyone stealing them."

"I didn't like them either, but Dino thought the paintings would attract attention since an Arabian Prince owns two of them."

"Yeah, because Roy gave him the first painting. It's true that the Prince paid for the second one. Don't ask me why he bought the second painting. Maybe he enjoys bidding on expensive things." I gave Irene a comforting pat on the back. "I really hate to see the Chihuly stuff go."

"Yeah, me too." She looked up at the driver of the chariot I'd been working on. "Is that Charlton Heston up there?"

I nodded.

She smiled and went inside.

My painters and I broke up the paint party a little early.

I drove in the direction of home but changed my mind and turned onto Main Street and then Freedom Boulevard. I drove to the Wells Fargo bank that Emmett liked so much, entered the building and spotted Gertrude right away. She nodded her head as I passed. She was working with a skinny, hunched over senior citizen, a woman wearing a large shawl over her head and half way down her ankle length dress. The profile looked familiar. It was Rusty's wife, Fahima.

At first it seemed odd that Gertrude and Fahima would be together, but the more I thought about it the more it wasn't a big deal. After all, Fahima had known Emmett for a zillion years and Gertrude had been married to Emmett's nephew years ago.

My mind moved on to the person I was looking for, Arnie. I spotted the weary sentinel leaning against the far wall next to the door leading to the safety deposit boxes. He looked semi-conscious, like he imagined he was miles away from the bank. Suddenly his ear phone alerted him to a call.

I glanced back at the teller window where Gertrude stood talking on a cell phone.

Fahima became impatient, using hand gestures to help make her point to Gertrude.

Arnie blinked himself into the moment and saw me coming.

I asked him to sit down with me for a minute. He said he could spare a little time, but not much. I understood how important his job was and knew he could give me lots of time if he wanted to. We sat down in the customer lounge area and chit chatted a bit. I said things like, "Why were you in Arizona?" He replied, "None of your business." I said, "Did you ever steal money from the German Club?" He lashed out with words I can't repeat, so I brought it down a notch.

"Is it true that your mother was Hilda's friend?"

"They played cards together."

"Do you play cards?"

"Are you kidding? That's for women and old men with nothing else to do," Arnie huffed.

"Have you ever been inside Emmett's house?"

"Yeah, once or twice—why?"

"Oh, just trying to understand Emmett's friends and acquaintances. Are you in the friend category?"

"No."

"What do you think of Emmett's nephew, Ed?"

"I think Gertrude was lucky to get away from that creep. If it weren't for their son Leroy, they wouldn't have a single thing in common."

"Does Gertrude see her son very often?"

"Sure, they go to dinner once a week…almost every week." He glanced at Gertrude. She didn't look happy. "I gotta get back to work."

I watched Arnie stroll back to the far wall where he braced himself for another half hour of boredom before the bank closed. On my way out, I saw Fahima tottering over to the front door. I stopped by Gertrude's window and greeted her with a sweet smile and a couple questions, like, "How are your cats?" She cocked her head to one side, probably wondering how I knew she had cats.

"My cats are fine, thank you." She picked up a folder, turned and marched ten steps over to a filing cabinet.

Unfortunately I came away from the bank with nothing new except that Arnie was not Emmett's friend, yet he'd been in the old man's house once or twice. What was that about? I would have to ask Emmett. I jumped into my truck and turned the key. Nothing happened. I tried again. Nothing. I was ready to call David when I looked up and saw an old guy in red and green high-water plaid slacks walking toward my pickup. Rusty stopped at the door. I rolled down the window.

"Hi, Rusty. Nice turtleneck. I'm glad you're here. Something is wrong with my truck."

"Josephine, I saw you from my car. Can I start your car for you?"

"Ah, sure." If you think you can, I thought.

Fahima tottered up to the truck and stood beside Rusty. Rusty found a latch and popped the hood open. He inspected everything, touching, tightening, tapping as he went. Finally he told me to start the engine. I tried and tried.

"Josephine, let me try," he said. We switched places, he turned the key and the truck started.

I thanked Rusty and told Fahima they should come over for dinner sometime. They smiled and agreed to come. I waved goodbye to the odd couple, Rusty who was stuck in the seventies and Fahima who still adhered to the customs of another country.

I cruised through the parking lot to Freedom Boulevard. Traffic was heavy on the Boulevard so I stopped at the grocery store to let the traffic die down before heading home.

Robert rang up my groceries. "Jo, I heard that an art gallery in Moss Landing got robbed."

"Yeah, it happens to be the gallery I'm working on."

"I heard they stole paintings by this famous artist, Roy something. There was a picture in the paper today of one of his paintings." Robert saw my grimace and laughed. "Pretty ugly if you ask me."

I carried my one bag of groceries to the truck, placed it in the passenger seat and hoped the engine would start. It did. Traffic had lightened up and I made it home in twenty minutes. I drove up my driveway and pulled to a stop behind an empty maroon Oldsmobile. Sunlight slanted in from the passenger window. I closed my eyes, took a couple deep breaths and tried to remember if I had invited Fahima and Rusty to dinner right away. What would I make for dinner?

David greeted me at the front door with a hug and funny grin. He leaned down, kissed my cheek and asked if I'd invited the folks to dinner.

I shrugged and said I guessed that I had. From there we went into action. David concocted a fabulous spaghetti ala marinara, created from two pounds of spaghetti, frozen meat, bottled marinara sauce and fresh garlic. I chopped lettuce, cabbage, onion and everything else I could find into a giant salad. We could have fed an army but instead we called the old folks to the dinning room table.

Fahima found her chair first.

Emmett and Rusty had been napping, but the smell of food must have rousted them. It wasn't a bad meal for being last minute. David had even whipped up a nice mousse for dessert.

I served cups of decaf while Rusty talked about his day.

Fahima was almost pleasant. I already knew the way to her heart, fast cars and lots of food.

"You must be proud of your nephew, Emmett," Rusty said. "I saw his picture in the paper. Too bad about the theft."

"You mean Leroy? What theft?"

"Yeah, he's not a loser any more," Rusty laughed.

"What do you mean by that?"

"You know, selling those paintings for thousands of dollars...."

"I don't know anything about that." Emmett took a sip of decaf.

Suddenly the room didn't exist. My mind skipped from Ed's house to Roy's apartment to a white van to something Dee had said in her phone call from the hospital. Something about Roy knowing where I lived. Roy's words came back to me, "Go back to Aromas..." Yes, he did know where I lived, but how? Why? In my mind I saw Leroy Hymiller's name spelled out. Drop the Le and the Hy and you have Roy Miller.

"Emmett, Rusty's right! Leroy Hymiller is calling himself Roy Miller. He's the artist who sold a painting to the Prince and his paintings were stolen from the Halikias Gallery."

Emmett took a minute to let my words sink in. "Yes, Josephine, now that I think about it, you could be right."

"Remember when Ed said he was happy because his son was finally making good money?"

Emmett nodded his head. "That explains why the picture in the newspaper looked so familiar. It looked very much like the paintings I bought from Leroy when he needed rent money a couple years ago. To me they all look alike."

"He has an unmistakable style," Rusty said.

"I know what you mean," I said, shifting in my chair. "Didn't someone steal the newspaper that day? I remember seeing a picture of Roy's painting in the paper that David brought over." My mind had gone into overdrive. Why would someone take my paper unless there was something in it we shouldn't see. Why would Leroy care if we saw his painting …?

"Josie, more coffee?" David asked.

I shook my head. "Emmett, the paintings you bought from your nephew were destroyed in the fire, right?"

"I suppose so. Like I said, I never hung them up because they looked sinister to me. We kept them in the basement." Emmett yawned, excused himself and headed for the loft.

Fahima's chin slid down and bounced off her chest a few times before Rusty decided she was sleepy and they needed to go home. I drove the Olds and David followed us in the Miata. Fahima seemed to be wide awake at that point, enjoying the ride while Rusty snored in the back seat.

When David and I were finally alone, driving home in his little sports car, I asked David what he thought about the discovery that Roy and Leroy were the same person.

"Some people change their name for business reasons. Maybe Leroy thought he could sell more paintings if his name was Roy Miller."

I rolled my eyes. "He could change it to DaVinci and no one would buy them."

CHAPTER TWENTY ONE

It was still dark outside Tuesday morning when I decided to get out of bed. I dressed for a day of mural painting, and stuffed a second set of clothes into a plastic bag along with a towel. My mind kept going back to the underwater scene of Solow in the deadly grip of a bicycle, bed springs and…. That was the scene I needed to clear up before reporting it to anyone. Did I really see what I thought I saw?

By the time Mr. Coffee produced his steamy drink, Hooley was up wondering why I was even awake at such an early hour. I told him I couldn't sleep because I was anxious to finish the Parthenon.

At the first glow of sunlight, I took Solow for a walk. We happened to end up at David's back door. I tapped on it and Solow lifted his head and howled.

David opened a glass door and poked his head out. "Josie, isn't it a little early for you…?"

"I wanted to get an early start today…kinda like a New Year's resolution—only later in the year." My face felt hot. I wasn't making sense. "I can't find my camera and I need to borrow yours."

David invited me in, yawned and stretched, pulled on a robe and then searched the hall closet for his camera. It was a quick search because his closet was nothing like mine. He handed over the little point-and-shoot tucked in a black strapped case. Other than being orange and blue, the camera looked quite ordinary, but I knew it was an underwater camera. A year ago I'd inadvertently dropped it in a tide pool when we were taking pictures of each other. David had told me not to worry because the camera was made for water.

Solow and I returned to my kitchen.

Emmett was hunched over the counter trying to crack an egg on the side of a bowl.

I took the egg and handed him a newspaper. My business could wait. Emmett needed all the calories I could give him, and I needed a few bites before I started my work day. The breakfast grew into pancakes with eggs and bacon, and no one can eat just a few bites of that, least of all, me.

I wore a pair of Bermuda shorts under my Levis. Between two pairs of pants and two helpings of pancakes, my mid-section was seriously squeezed. I pointed my pickup toward Moss Landing, the camera and bag of clothes riding in the passenger seat with my purse.

It was eight-thirty when I parked in front of Bill's, the last place I wanted to be. I sat for a moment, staring at foamy salt water splashing against a bank of boulders. My heart beat a little faster just thinking about cold murky water. I looked at the road, no one there, Bill's deck, no one there. The fishing boats were already out on the bay and the town looked empty.

A seal barked.

I jumped.

I talked to myself about sticking to the plan, kicked off my flip flops and wiggled out of my jeans. I crossed over a few yards of cold granite rocks to the water's edge. I sat for a minute with my legs in the water, hoping to acclimate. That didn't happen so I slipped into the surf with the camera strapped around my neck. The murky part was worse than I remembered.

I did a sort of dog-paddle breaststroke, angling down to the junk pile some ten feet below the surface. I pointed the camera, saw the bed springs and clicked. I worked my way around the trash for a different angle and took another picture, came up for air and returned for a couple more pictures. I came up for more air again and went down one last time to really look at the stuff below. A stack of painted canvases sat on the sandy bottom with bed springs and a bicycle piled on top.

I swam to the shore and looked up. Alicia bent down to give me a hand.

"Thank…you…Allie."

"I saw your truck and wondered what you were doing here. I'm still wondering. You look exhausted, Jo. Did you swim across the slough?"

"No, just some snooping around over there." I pointed to the spot.

"I guess you'll tell me all about it…."

I did tell her everything, right after I dried off and changed into dry clothes. The storage shed beside the gallery worked nicely as a changing room. A smear of lipstick and I was good as new—except for the smell of rotting kelp.

Alicia could hardly believe my story. We talked about Roy's paintings until Kyle arrived. He helped lay out the tarps and set up the ladders. Once we were situated on our ladders, Allie joyfully told me her exciting news.

"My family—my sister and her daughter—are coming to dinner tomorrow night. I'm practically jumping out of my skin, I'm so excited."

"I'm so happy for you, Allie. They're going to love the lady you've become."

"Thanks. I was hoping you might drop in, you know, in case things are awkward or uncomfortable."

"I can't imagine that. But I'll drop in. I can't wait to meet them."

We discussed Alicia's dinner menu, flowers, clothes, and then agreed that she didn't have to try to impress anyone. Trigger would instantly sweep them off their feet.

After lunch, an insurance adjuster met with Nico and Irene. I wanted to be in the conversation, but it was too early. I needed to print the pictures I took before making any accusations. My head sorted and resorted bits of information. Why would someone purposely hide paintings in ten feet of water.

"Jo, how come your chariot has five wheels?" Kyle asked in passing.

"Oops, I'll just paint over that."

At four o'clock I told my friends to clean the brushes and go home. All I could think about was David. I could hardly wait to show David the pictures. Actually, he would see them with me because he had a printer and I didn't. I drove up his driveway full of anticipation, but I didn't see his Jeep. I peeked in the garage window. The Miata was inside. I tried the door. Locked! I ran to the backyard and tried the sliding-glass doors. Rats!

I sat in the cab of my truck and called David on his cell phone. He answered right away, letting me know he was with Emmett and they were touring a house across the street from mine. The "for sale" sign had been up for a couple days and David had mentioned he wanted to see what the house was like.

I parked in my driveway beside the Jeep and walked across the street to the ranch-style house with a "for sale" sign. The guys had their hands up, leaning against a large picture window. I joined them, forgetting all about the photos. It looked like no one was home, but I rang the bell anyway to make sure.

We wandered to the back of the house and peeked in several windows. The inside looked clean and tidy, like the yard. We guessed it was around 2,500 square feet and had a cute little house in the rear under the trees. It looked like a roomy granny-unit.

Emmett liked the garage because half of it had been turned into a shop featuring overhead sky-lights and a long workbench.

"I bet you could build a lot of clocks in this shop," David said as they peeked in a window.

"Yes I could, and the shelving looks sturdy enough."

I began to see a pattern. David pointed out all the good things about the property, setting up Emmett to think about them. David should have earned a commission on his sales pitch. We'd discussed Emmett's next home earlier in the week. We both wanted it to be close by, with room for a vegetable garden and a workshop.

Emmett had received a check from his insurance company about ten days ago. He talked about rebuilding his house until he saw this one. His check was more than enough to pay for this lovely stucco house with terra cotta tiles on the roof and pond in the back. There was plenty of room for Lilly and Solow to romp and play.

Emmett said he would make an offer on the house.

David and I looked at each other—our eyes did a "high five." It would be wonderful to have Emmett settled into his own home close to us. I mentally crossed my fingers and then my toes for even more luck. We crossed the street, trudged up my driveway and found Solow sleeping on the porch.

"David, I need a favor. I need to use your printer."

"Sure, go ahead." He fished around in a pocket for his keys and handed them to me.

"Except, I need you to help me." My expertise in computers and printers was minimal to say the least. I strapped the camera around my neck.

"No problem. See you later, Emmett." David helped me into the Jeep. Solow went into the house with Emmett.

Two minutes later we entered David's house. "OK, what's this all about," he asked.

"The pictures will tell you what it's about."

David plugged the camera into his computer and downloaded four pictures. There it was on the screen, a pile of junk in murky water.

"Josie, what am I looking at? It looks like these were taken underwater."

"Yep. See the bike and the bed springs and then look down here. Do you see the corner of something sticking out? That is a painting...probably five of them. I think those are the paintings stolen from the gallery. I'm wondering if the painter did this for the insurance money." My heart did a double thump at the thought.

"I think I see what you're talking about. Is that a jelly fish?"

"Don't look at the fish. Look at the canvases. Maybe if you print the pictures they'll be easier to see."

"OK, Sweetie. There's the first one. You're right, something is under that junk." He printed the other three pictures, all murky like the first.

The first picture was enough evidence for me, but another scenario crossed my mind.

David played with my hair and pressed his lips to my neck. He was feeling frisky and I needed to get home. He was tender and sweet as I contemplated my next dive into the sea. I could go to Irene and Nico with the photos, but it would be even better if I recovered the actual paintings. I'd leave the house early in the morning, tie a rope to the springs and the other end to the truck pumper. It happened without a hitch, in my head. In reality, it wasn't so easy.

Wednesday, eight a.m. I drove to Moss Landing semi-confident that I could recover the paintings. I had rope in the truck bed and a plan in my head. I parked the truck in front of Bill's, peeled off my jeans, kicked off my flip flops and hauled the twenty-five-foot rope to the water's edge. I forced myself into the chilly water, took a huge breath and swam down to the junk pile. I quickly tied the rope onto a bed spring and rushed to the surface. I gulped air and swam the short distance to shore.

Sopping wet and freezing cold, I hoisted my body onto the rocks and hauled the rope to the front end of my truck. When the rope was securely tied to the bumper, I climbed into the cab, revved the motor and dropped it into reverse. At first the truck barely moved. I gave it more gas. Suddenly it moved fast— very fast and stopped even faster against something solid with a loud crash of metal-on-metal. I cranked my head around and saw a shocked face with ice blue eyes staring back. My truck had melded into the deputy's back seat—trunk area. Deputy Sayer didn't look happy either. He came to my door with gun in hand.

"Step out."

I climbed out and stood on wobbly legs, shivering and speechless. Out of the corner of my eye, I saw bed springs perched on a giant granite rock. I almost smiled.

"Ms. Stuart, do you think this is funny?"

"No, of course not. But look, the springs. I got em!"

"Ma'am, have you been drinking?"

"It's eight-thirty in the morning. Why would I be drinking? See those springs? I did that."

"You are confessing...."

"No, I'm telling you who stole paintings from the gallery. Honest, the paintings are still down there, but I had to move the springs and bicycle to get at them."

Just then a canvas miraculously surfaced.

Sayer's jaw dropped. He slowly holstered his weapon, keeping his eyes on the painting.

Lund temporarily lost her scowl.

As we watched, the tide sloshed the big canvas to shore and slammed it against the rocks. The second time it encountered the rocks, Deputy Sayer snatched it out of the water. He noted the signature and showed it to us.

"I'm pretty sure there are four more paintings down there," I said.

Another canvas surfaced and then another. We pulled them out one-by-one, as soon as they sloshed against the rocks with the tide. Lund caught the fourth and I pulled in the fifth painting, all signed by R. M. While the deputies radioed for a new car and then put their heads together trying to figure out what to do with me, I dried myself off and used the towel to wipe seaweed and scum off the paintings. They were not even damaged. Sayer said they'd be turned into "evidence."

I watched Alicia's Volvo creep around the Sheriff's smashed up car and park a block away at the gallery.

Kyle buzzed by the cruiser a few minutes later and parked next to Alicia. My painters began their paint-day without me.

CHAPTER TWENTY-TWO

It was noon before the deputies cut me loose. I had answered their questions to the best of my knowledge, and Deputy Sayer wrote down every word. The three of us moseyed down the block to the gallery where Irene and Nico were notified about the discovery of five of the seven stolen paintings. Like me, they thought of insurance money as a reason to steal and only one person would benefit from the theft—the artist himself.

Deputy Lund wanted to know where Roy lived. I told her Roy had recently moved but I didn't know where. I wanted to tell her my theory about the paintings being stolen twice, once from Emmett and again from the gallery, but without proof I had nothing. If they couldn't find Roy by next Tuesday, I had a pretty good idea how to locate him—if he didn't flee the country.

In the meantime, I had a mural to finish and dinner at Alicia's to look forward to. The painting started late and broke up early for me. By four o'clock I smelled strongly of sweat, seaweed and ugly murky water residue. Kyle kindly told me so. If that wasn't bad enough, my hair looked like a troll had styled it using diesel oil.

Driving home was a joy. I had uncovered a thief, crashed into a cop car without hurting my truck badly and I was fairly certain Emmett had found his new home. In fact, he was on the phone with his realtor when I walked into the house.

Emmett's call ended. He told me he'd made an offer on the house across the street and his realtor sounded optimistic about his chances. There were other bidders, but she said his offer sounded good—very clean with a thirty-day escrow.

"If you get the house, what are you going to do with the cottage?"

"Live in it."

"Huh?"

"I live in a loft right now, and I don't mind it at all. I want to live in a small house. I've been doing a lot of thinking, thanks to David. I'm beginning to see that Ed has a real problem with Rose and a worse problem with his son. I'm going to ask Ed if he'd like to rent the big house for the same price he's paying for his apartment. I'd have the shop, of course. Maybe I can help him with his book and he'll help me when I get old. That's how families are supposed to be."

"That's wonderful, Hooley! Did you decide all this today?"

"David helped me to sort things out. Why are you not married to that good man?"

I blushed. "We're in no hurry."

"You better hurry. How long do you think I'll be around for the wedding?" he laughed.

Trying to hide my school-girl blush, I trotted off to the shower, double scrubbed everything and came out sparkling clean. I dried, fluffed and sprayed my hair, polished my nails and pulled on my best slacks and silk shirt.

"Josephine, you look brand new. And you smell good too."

"Thank you, Emmett; you're a 'lady killer' yourself. I'm going to Alicia's for dinner tonight. Will you be all right here, alone?"

"I won't be alone. David and I are going to watch a basketball game on the television and drink beer."

"Really."

"Solow will be here too so you don't have to worry about me. David showed me the pictures you took of my nephew's paintings. I recognized three of them. They used to be in my basement. The boy is a bad seed, a disgrace to the family...."

"I wondered if that was the case. I don't know what to say...." My heart went out to Emmett, and at the same time raced at the thought of being right about Roy/Leroy, whatever, stealing the paintings he'd sold to Hooley years ago. I wished it could have been a stranger, but at the same time, I was ecstatic that we knew who the killer was.

"Have you told anyone? Does David know?"

"I didn't tell David. I wanted to tell you first, Josephine. You've been working very hard to find Hilda's murderer. You should be the one to tell the police."

"Actually, the Sheriff's Deputies are looking for your nephew right now. They're pretty sure he stole the paintings from the gallery. I hope Leroy doesn't come around here looking for trouble."

"Say no more. Go to your party and have some fun. We'll be fine."

I gave Solow a quick ear rub, kissed Emmett on the cheek and walked to my truck. The tailgate looked a little wrinkled and a taillight was missing. But that was nothing compared to the T-boned cruiser. My sweet little truck sailed toward Watsonville as if nothing had happened to it. I arrived at the Quintana's early. Alicia seemed happy that I had and put me to work setting the table. Trigger and I always got the simple jobs.

I decided not to tell anyone about Emmett's nephew until I had time to contact the police. If I'd called them after talking to Emmett, I'd have missed Alicia's reunion with her family. I wanted to support her any way I could.

Ernie and Alicia hustled around in the kitchen, slicing, pouring, stirring, and tasting.

"Ernie, I hear a car!" Alicia dropped what she was doing, ran through the living room and opened the front door.

I looked up when I heard a familiar voice, and stepped into the living room. Two lovely women walked through the doorway. The first lady looked like she was in her mid-forties. She wore her black hair short. Her dress was the latest style and her two-inch heels brought her up to five-foot-nine.

The second woman was a speck taller and beautiful as usual with her trim figure and one blue eye.

I couldn't believe my eyes. What was Dee doing at Alicia's party? Was she invited too?

As Alicia and Eva hugged and cried, it suddenly occurred to me that Dee was actually Eva's daughter, Dolores. I stood back and watched the very touching reunion, wiping tears back with my hand and smiling until it hurt.

As I had predicted, the two women loved Trigger immediately.

Alicia glowed as she introduced her sister and niece to me.

Dee and I laughed and hugged. It was good to see her so happy. All eyes were on us.

"You two act like you know each other," Alicia said. "What's going on?"

"Remember that crazy story I told you about a cave in Arizona?"

"You mean that really ha...I mean, Dolores is the student who saved you?"

"That's right. I can't wait to talk to her about something...." Everyone headed for Ernie in the kitchen, except Dee because I hung onto her sleeve. "Dee, do you know Roy's new address...or what town...or anything?"

"No, what's the creep done now? Did I tell you my turquoise squash blossom necklace was missing after that awful visit at Roy's place in Capitola?"

"No, you didn't tell me." I was stunned. "Roy has been up to worse than that lately!"

"This morning I read an article in the paper about Roy's paintings being stolen from the gallery."

"Yeah, but he's the one who stole them—probably for the insurance money."

Dee rolled her eyes. "What a jerk." She left me and found her way to the kitchen.

I followed, but just as an observer in the doorway. The kitchen could hardly hold all the happiness, laughter and tears bouncing around. Eva and Alicia looked a lot alike and had their whole lives to talk about. Trigger was crazy about Dee and she obviously loved her cousin.

I disappeared into the living room, picked up my purse and left with a smile.

The sun had already hit the turf, but the sky still had plenty of bright sunset colors in it when I arrived at my home. The boys were into the game, so I called Solow to the kitchen where we shared leftover chicken enchiladas and ice cream. It had been a long time since my buddy and I spent quality time and calories together.

The next day was Wednesday, a good day to call the Deputies and invite them over for an enlightening conversation.

I called early, they arrived at noon.

Deputy Lund's eyes didn't seem as cold as I remembered. I offered her a seat on the couch. Deputy Sayer sat down beside her. Emmett sat in the rocker and I took the ottoman. I let Emmett do the talking since his credibility was not in question. They listened to him and then Deputy Sayer began the questioning.

"Mr. Hooley, do you have any proof that your nephew sold the paintings to you?"

"Sure, Ed was there. It was his idea...."

"To cheat you?"

"No, no, Ed thought it would help his son's career as a painter. A sale would encourage him to paint more and better I guess. I wanted to help too. I paid him but I never hung the paintings."

"Why not?"

"I didn't like them. They made me feel... uncomfortable."

"Did Leroy know that you didn't like his paintings, in other words, did you give him reason to not like you?"

"No, I never gave him a reason to hate me. But I'm sure he likes money," Emmett sighed as his head dropped into his hands.

"I hope you don't have any more questions," I said. "As you can see, Mr. Hooley is very tired."

"We'll put out an all-points bulletin on Mr. Hymiller right away," Deputy Lund said as she stood and walked to the door.

"You'll let us know when you catch him?"

Deputy Sayer nodded and walked out the door behind Ms. Blue Eyes.

The deputies didn't call for the next five days. We finished the mural Friday and the Chihuly collection came back to the gallery, David and I went on an actual date Saturday night, Emmett and I visited Ed on

Sunday and I cleaned house Monday. When Tuesday rolled around, I knew what I had to do. I told the boys a big fib. I said I was meeting Alicia for a movie downtown.

Tuesday nights are pretty quiet in Capitola Village. The locals have their choice of a dozen or more fantastic restaurants, and they take advantage of early-bird specials. I arrived in town just before five in case my prey liked an early dinner. I curbed my truck in front of the Mom & Pop Diner and waited.

Two hours went by. My stomach growled.

Finally I gave in to my hunger, entered the restaurant and ordered a burger to go. I watched a young couple and a family of five stand up and leave. Only three tables still had customers. I wondered if the burgers were any good and looked around the room to see if anyone had ordered one. Out of the corner of my eye I saw a couple coming up the sidewalk. The door opened and the woman entered first. By that time, I was halfway down the hall and into the lady's room.

My heart beat frantically as I pulled my cell phone from my purse. I dialed 911 and whispered my message to the emergency operator. She said her name was Michelle and would I please speak louder and calm down.

"Roy Miller, I mean Leroy Hymiller is in a restaurant in Capitola. He's wanted for murder!" I hissed. "Please, send police—anybody, before he gets away."

"Stay on the line Ma'am. I have a police unit on the way. Where are you?"

"In the bathroom...."

"The address, Ma'am."

"Um, it's Bay Avenue, the Mom & Pop Diner next to the surfboard shop."

"Can you ask someone for the number?"

I poked my head out the door and looked down the hallway. I saw the waitress, but I also saw the party in question sitting at the bar just twenty feet from where I stood. I quietly closed the door.

"Are you still there, Ma'am?"

"I'm here," I whispered, "I can't leave the restroom without being seen. Tell the police to hurry!"

"Can you describe the person wanted for murder?"

"He's tall, thin, could use some sun—you know, way too white with black curly hair and he's wearing a black t-shirt and he's with a tall silver-haired lady, his stepmother actually, and she's wearing a black pantsuit and a turquoise...." Suddenly someone opened the bathroom door, jamming it against my hip. I pushed it closed but not before we saw each other in the mirror.

"She saw me—she knows I'm here. Hurry!" I could barely catch my breath. Should I try to stop them from leaving? Michelle kept talking but my mind was spinning—trying to think of a way to stop the thieving murderer. "Oh, there's a little window...." I put the phone in my pocket.

"Hello? Are you there?" came Michelle's muffled voice.

I climbed from the toilet onto the sink, unlatched the ancient tinted-glass window and raised it as far as it would go. I dropped my purse out the window. Luckily I hadn't eaten the burger I ordered. The window was a tight fit, and every millimeter counted. Crouched in the sink, I contorted my body around until my derriere faced the fence outside. One leg stretched out and down. The second one wasn't easy, but eventually both legs dangled while my body stubbornly slithered backwards out the window.

Michelle tried and tried to call me to the phone, but my phone was in my back pocket and out of reach.

Bam! Metal-on-metal, as my feet kicked over two bicycles and a blue Weber. I let go of the window sill and landed on top of everything. A handlebar pressed against my ribs. I stepped down onto a long narrow slab of cracked concrete bordered by tall wooden fencing and ran to a gate at one end, swung the bolt up and let myself out.

Capitola looked like it was asleep, even thought the sky was brilliant yellow and orange going red. I listened for voices but only heard waves pounding the shore two blocks away, or was that my heart pounding in my ears? I climbed into my truck and watched—of all people—Rose and Roy through the front window. Maybe Rose hadn't recognized me. They seemed to be enjoying their meal and a conversation with the waitress.

Minutes ticked by, no police.

The sky darkened along with my spirits. If Roy decided to leave I'd have to stop him somehow.

He paid his bill.

I fired up the truck.

Roy and Rose stood up to leave.

I flipped on the headlights.

They walked toward the door.

I backed up three car-lengths, made a wide half circle ending with my truck jumping the curb. Engine breath touched the glass door entrance to the restaurant. My heart pounded.

Roy stood frozen, slack-jawed, starring into the headlights.

A far away siren became louder and then there was silence.

A policeman leaped out, gun drawn and shouted for me to get out of my vehicle.

I showed him my empty hands and climbed out of the cab. "Officer, I did this on purpose…."

"I can see that," he said as his partner pulled my hands back and cuffed them.

"You don't understand…Roy Miller, I mean Leroy Hymiller is wanted for murder."

While one officer made sure I didn't move from my standing-cuffed position, the other one backed my truck away from the door.

Stupefied, Roy stood glued to the floor, staring at us through the glass.

"That's him!" I shouted.

The officer guarding me looked into Roy's pale grimacing face.

Rose, wearing Dee's turquoise necklace, suddenly came out of her trance, grabbed Roy's arm and pulled him out to the sidewalk.

"He's wanted for the murder of Hilda Hymiller… you have to believe me…. Don't let him get away!"

The policeman let go of my arm and stepped up to the exiting couple. "Sir, your name please."

"Ah, Roy Miller, ask anybody." Sweat drizzled down his forehead.

The second officer joined our little group. "Roy Miller, huh. Alias for Leroy Hymiller. Cuff him!"

"You can't do that," Rose shouted, sending the full force of her body directly into the first officer, who happened to be shorter and lighter than his attacker.

The officer steadied himself, quickly twirled her around and cuffed her.

"It's not Leroy's fault," Rose cried. "I gave him the idea to steal the paintings. Emmett never even hung them up. He wouldn't miss them anyway. They were worth a fortune."

"Get in the car, Ma'am."

"I'm happy to go to jail. It can't be any worse than where I live now."

"What about the diamond jewelry? And why did he have to blow the place up?" I snapped.

"Get in the car, Ma'am," the first officer snarled.

"You don't understand—Emmett and Hilda hoarded all that wealth," she screamed as they stuffed her into the cruiser.

Just before the door slammed, I shouted, "Wait till Dee finds out you have her necklace."

Cop number two told cop number one to un-cuff me and then he warned me to get my taillight fixed. Not a big thing in my world at that moment. I felt like the Capitola Mall had been lifted off my shoulders. Emmett would be safe and I'd enjoy more time with David. Life was good and I couldn't wait to go home and tell the boys all about it.

EPILOGUE

Funny how quickly major excitement can dissipate, leaving one to question whether the event really happened. But I knew it really happened. I knew Leroy and Rose were in jail, with their pictures on the front page of the *Sentinel*. But how in the world was Rose able to have dinner with Leroy every Tuesday night? I read a little more about the unlucky couple. It seems Rose was allowed to leave the institution for a couple hours every Tuesday as long as Leroy took responsibility for her safety, and because evil attracts evil, they came up with a plan to acquire fame and fortune.

As soon as the police investigation was completed, Kat hit the road, wanting nothing to do with the captured couple. After a long interview with the police, even they didn't know what she knew and when she knew it. Tight lips had served her well. I hoped I would never run into her again.

Rose was the big mouth, telling the police how Leroy had carted the paintings and jewelry out of Emmett's house, turned the gas stove on, waited a while outside and then lit a long fuse attached to a firecracker. The explosion knocked him to the ground, but he managed to drive away before the second blast, when the propane tank exploded. Giving Leroy evil ideas was the perfect revenge.

According to the police, Hilda died in her sleep, not wearing her hearing aid and not knowing that her nephew was prowling her bedroom for jewelry

I pushed the prickly pair out of my mind and thought about my best friend, Alicia, and her new-found family. I'd never seen her so happy. Her older sister would always stay close, but Dee was another story. Anyone could see that she was the adventurous one in the family.

Emmett was like family to me. Helping him move into his new digs had me puffy-eyed with a knot in my throat. Most of my tears were happy tears because my friend wasn't going very far away. He had bought the house across the street. Ed would live in the main house and watch over Emmett who planned to live in the back yard cottage, right next to a miniature cottage and pen for Lilly.

Once Emmett was settled into his new home, Solow and I came by for a visit. I knew right away that Emmett was doing well. He had color in his cheeks, a contented smile and had already gained a few pounds. He told me how good it felt to have Ed in the big house, writing his book and sharing his home-cooked gourmet meals. He mowed the lawn, took out the garbage and paid the rent. Ed was not a slacker as I'd been led to believe.

A few weeks after Leroy and Rose's capture, I drove Emmett to the gallery—"the Parthenon" as people were starting to call it. Irene and Nico loved the attention the mural brought to the newspapers and the public. Emmett walked up to the first faux column and touched it to make sure it was just a flat wall and not a real pillar. We toured the inside, admiring the Chihuly glass collection, Bonni's newest paintings and, of course, the giant mermaid. On the way home, I dropped Hooley off at his old property for a last look before the new owners took it over.

The up-side of Emmett leaving was that I was seeing more of David. David was grateful to have me back on planet earth instead of bouncing around the country trying to find Hilda's murderer.

The day before Emmett moved out of my house, he presented me with a magnificent cuckoo clock. A colorful, traditionally dressed couple chased a rascally bear out of their chalet every fifteen minutes while the cuckoo popped in and out of his window noisily. Emmett had assembled the clock using parts and figures gathered from the floor of his old cottage after the explosion. He signed the back of the clock with, "Dearest Josephine, I am forever grateful."

Happily, I tossed my old plastic clock in the trash, hung my lovely new cuckoo clock on the wall and watched the tiny creatures go through their gyrations. I couldn't help smiling at their unrelenting energy and joy, maybe because, for the first time in a long time, I felt the same way. Thank you too, Emmett.

THE END

ABOUT THE AUTHOR

 As a retired muralist and commercial artist, Joyce Oroz has an abundance of painting experiences she infuses into Josephine's adventures. Oroz say, "Writing is like painting a series of pictures without the messy paint." She spends her time writing mysteries, a blog and monthly newspaper articles. She is happily settled in Aromas, California, with her husband, also a writer, and their Labrador retriever. CUCKOO CLOCK CAPER is her first mystery with Cozy Cat Press.